Rabbit - Text copyright © Emmy Ellis 2024
Cover Art by Emmy Ellis @ studioenp.com © 2024

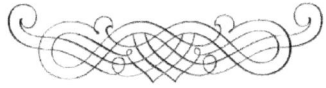

All Rights Reserved

Rabbit is a work of fiction. All characters, places, and events are from the author's imagination. Any resemblance to persons, living or dead, events or places is purely coincidental.

The author respectfully recognises the use of any and all trademarks.

With the exception of quotes used in reviews, this book may not be reproduced or used in whole or in part by any means existing without written permission from the author.

Warning: The unauthorised reproduction or distribution of this copyrighted work is illegal. No part of this book may be scanned, uploaded, or distributed via the Internet or any other means, electronic or print, without the author's written permission.

RABBIT

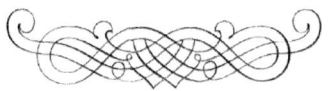

Emmy Ellis

Chapter One

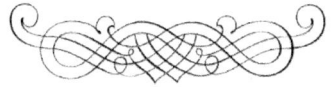

Ichabod Ahearn sat in the big house he'd visited when he'd been on surveillance watching the now-dead leader, Goldie, a fair old while back. It seemed different here somehow, although everything *looked* like it had before. The air of the place wasn't the same. It buzzed with something he couldn't define. Anxiety? Anticipation? Anger? He imagined the latter played a big role inside the woman sitting opposite him. Perhaps bewilderment along with a sense of betrayal. He felt for her, what she was going through. If he had the guts, he'd offer her a hug, but he didn't, so that was that. He told himself to keep a respectful distance unless he sensed she needed the touch of someone who cared, but even then he'd likely hold back. Because this was the woman he fancied, and he was crap when it came to women. Besides, some people were prickly when they'd been hurt, and he didn't want to add to her troubles.

Marleigh Jasper had phoned The Brothers to tell them her husband, David, was bringing drugs into the country, and everything had changed for Ichabod. But that might be because he'd fancied her ever since he'd set eyes on her but couldn't have her, and maybe he could now. Maybe, because she'd grassed her man up, she wouldn't want him in her life anymore.

Maybe Ichabod had a chance.

He almost laughed at the thought.

Ye're livin' in cloud cuckoo land.

She'd made tea, and they sat in her expensive, gleaming kitchen at the island. This place was such a far cry from the flat he rented off The

Brothers. He received good wages for working at Jackpot Palace, plus surveillance jobs, but he was happy where he lived. Didn't need the flat for anything other than sleeping and showering because he was a workaholic.

It took his mind off certain things.

Had he fixated on Marleigh so *she* took his mind off things, too?

God, she was lovely. He'd often pictured them together, and halfway through the fantasies of them going on dates, he convinced himself she wouldn't want to be with *him*, a crass Irishman, so what was the point in hoping he'd bag the pot of gold at the end of the much-wanted rainbow? But they'd got along well enough when she'd sat with him back then, and she'd fed him, kept his thirst at bay with many cuppas. A kind woman, lonely, one who didn't deserve to be left by herself for long stretches.

She was older than him, though, not that it mattered to him, but it might to her. He reckoned she held keeping up appearances in high regard. A trait he wasn't fond of.

Ichabod's first encounter with her came about because she'd contacted George and Greg about Goldie, saying how she and David had seen a woman at the window above the leader's tanning shop, Golden Glow, who seemed desperate for help. Marleigh had phoned the police, who hadn't done anything about it, and when news came later, regarding a woman refugee found dead, she'd put two and two together. At the time, Ichabod had thought David was as pure as his wife, wanting any other women kept safe, but he must have been hiding his true self.

Feckin' sneaky bastard.

Or was there another reason he'd turned into a drug mule?

Drugs. They brought on reminders of the past, that time in Ireland Ichabod tried so hard to forget. But his part in that story, his wicked, wicked part, would never leave him. What he'd done was—

Ye had no choice, remember that.

He blinked, forcing himself back into the present.

"Are you okay?" Marleigh asked.

"Yeah, just lost myself for a second."

"I know how that goes."

Once Marleigh eventually told him her story today, he had one of his own to tell. About Katy Marlborough, a woman he despised, but he shoved that aside for the minute. First, he wanted to take in Marleigh's presence, her beauty, how she was so poised and elegant despite the turmoil she must be going through. He wanted to get to know the *real* her, the one who lived beneath the surface. Although he shouldn't stare at her like some lovesick eejit. She'd think he was weird.

He smiled at her. "The twins have told me what they know, but I'd like tae hear it from ye."

Those words. Someone else had said similar to *him*, when *he'd* been the one having to recall his story. That week in Ireland. The events that upset him while he slept sometimes, appearing as vivid nightmares. During the waking hours, especially at the casino, he sometimes saw people who looked like those in Ireland, and he did a double-take to make sure it wasn't them. He didn't want certain folks being here, knowing about his life, what he did. Because then they'd realise he'd played a massive part back then.

That he was a killer.

Marleigh sighed. Was it tinged with anger or sadness? "As I told you before, David goes away a lot for his job. Abroad. I went with him sometimes, but not often. Now I understand why. The times I *could* go, he wasn't bringing in drugs.

I thought he was a decent man. Never in a million years would I have put him down as…as who he is. Drugs? It's disgusting. So many lives are ruined by them."

Aye, they feckin' are. "Yet ye turned tae people who allow them tae be sold on their Estate."

She blushed. "I…um…I can overlook that. The twins are good men deep down. Please don't muddy the waters by reminding me of what they're involved in. I can only handle so much at once. My life has turned on its head, and I'm struggling to deal with it."

"Sorry. I didn't mean tae upset ye." He changed the subject to prompt her to move on, although no subject in this conversation would skirt around what had happened. "So ye spent Christmas alone."

"Unfortunately, yes. I *did* ask him why he couldn't be home, why he had to work over the break, which he's never done before, but he said it was unavoidable, gave me no other explanation."

"How did ye find out what he was up tae?"

Her long blonde hair shimmered in a shaft of winter sunlight coming in through the window. It was the morning after Boxing Day, and David would be back tomorrow. George and Greg were busy sorting out a sting operation, and it involved Marleigh. She wasn't aware of that yet, but she would be.

She rested her arms on the island and smoothed a fingertip over one of her shiny manicured nails. Coral-coloured. As pretty as her. "Well, after he'd said it was unavoidable and had left the house, I went snooping. I was fed up of him being so evasive when it came to his job. It's always bugged me why he has a safe at home he *said* was private and only for work, and I understand I can't see any documents, but it seemed, I don't know, shifty. *Too* secretive."

"How did ye get into it, the safe?"

She rolled her eyes. "It seems he's not as clever as he thinks. He used my birthdate as the unlock code."

"What, exactly, did ye find?"

"A schedule. In a ledger. He'd even been so silly as to put words like *cocaine* and *heroin*. The dates went back quite a while, and I married them with my diary—they were the times he went away. Starting three years ago, when he began going on his trips. I'd written about how sketchy he was being; it had bothered me enough to do that. Back then, I'd asked why he needed to even go away when he hadn't before. His role didn't fit with having to speak to investors or whatever in person. And what was wrong with the video calls he used to be on anyway? I thought about other reasons why he kept leaving. A week later, I'd put in my diary that I was just being paranoid, that he wasn't having an affair."

Anger burned Ichabod. Affairs hurt a lot of people. "*That's* what ye thought he was up tae at first?"

"Yes."

"But ye told me ye were in love, that ye trusted him wid ye life."

She blinked a few times. Blushed again. "People lie to cover the hurts inside. To make out everything is okay."

That struck a chord on so many levels, and he nodded, but again it was a reminder of how she wanted to keep up appearances. People in Ireland had done that, but the truth had come out in the end. Years later, but still. "Ye could have confided in me. I wouldn't have passed it on tae anyone."

"I know, but I was ashamed for being the woman who did as she was told, the one who didn't question anything once David had given an explanation."

"Which was?"

"That his boss, Harry, had chosen him as the face-to-face man of the company and that was the end of it. Nothing he could do if he wanted to keep his job. There were others who could take his place easily. In other words, he had to do as he was instructed or find another position elsewhere."

"Do ye think he lied about that?"

"Maybe."

"Do ye think he's bringin' drugs in for Harry?"

She laughed. "I doubt it. I found out he *did* have to go away for work, so that wasn't a lie. I've been to parties where his boss was present, and we chatted about David being away. Although..." She paused, thinking. "Harry frowned at me when I said David was off on a plane more than he was at home. I realise now he must have thought that was odd. I wish he'd said something in front of David so I could have seen his reaction."

"So even though ye told yeself everythin' was above board, ye still questioned his boss' frown. That tells me ye were suspicious no matter what."

She stared across at the window. She looked like a painting, so still and perfect. "You can tell yourself not to be suspicious, but the mind has a nasty way of not shutting up."

I know.

She continued. "Once an affair was in my head, I couldn't get it out. It wasn't always at the forefront of my mind, though."

"And ye stayed wid David despite ye worries."

"I did."

"Ye carried on, wid *everythin'*?" This part of the story had strands of the past in it, a past Ichabod hadn't known about until his cousin, Rowan, had come over from Ireland to work at Jackpot Palace.

"Sex, you mean?" Her top lip curled, as if she was disgusted with herself now. She faced him. "You have to understand that when he came home, after I'd questioned him about whatever trip he'd been on and his answers were plausible, it all went back to normal. Him being here erased my fears. He acted the same, going to work, coming home at the right time. We went on dates, he treated me well. It wasn't until he mentioned going away again that those fears resurfaced, reminding me what he could be getting up to."

Once, when Ichabod had sat at her bedroom window watching Goldie's house, Marleigh had been asleep in the bed behind him. He'd had a thought, that David led a dual life, which was why she couldn't go away with him all the time. Even though they knew he was dabbling in drugs, could that still be true? Another woman?

"Why did ye put yeself through it?" he asked.

She stared down at the island top. "Because I didn't want my perfect bubble to burst. If I'd asked him if he was up to anything, what would I have done if he'd said yes? It would have forced me to face things I didn't want to."

Ichabod frowned. He hadn't thought Marleigh was the type to stay with a man because of the life he could provide, a user, a gold-digger. She didn't have to work, there was plenty of money on hand, and now he worried his view of her could be tainted if she revealed more about herself. That his flawless rendering of her, the one that filled his thoughts every day, could have stains splashed all over it. But who was he to cast aspersions? He hadn't exactly been the perfect person, had he. He'd made choices to suit his situation. He'd used people.

He wanted to get right inside her mind. To understand her. "*Why* didn't ye ask him? Tell me the *real* reason."

She lifted her head, her eyes glassy with tears. "Shame, I suppose. Everyone in our circle finding out I was the last to know. The thought of them all laughing at me behind my back. And he was still attentive, still acted as if he loved me."

"Maybe he did. Does. Maybe he wasn't havin' it away wid anyone else because he was too busy bringin' drugs into London. That could be all that was. It doesn't excuse him lyin' tae ye, though."

She huffed out a laugh. "But how could he tell me what he was doing? He knows I would have gone to the police."

"But ye didn't, ye chose The Brothers. Why?"

"Because of how effectively they dealt with things regarding Goldie."

"Killin' him, ye mean." He pushed out a long breath. "So ye want David dead for what he's done?"

"No, I just…I just want the twins to question him, find out who he's working for on the side. What if it's a nasty outfit and they come for me? I'm alone here most of the time. What if he does something they don't like and they punish *me* for it to teach him a lesson?"

Ichabod needed to know how she'd feel if David had been *forced* to bring drugs in. To know where he stood with her, if anywhere.

Feck it, I went and got my hopes up when the twins told me about this. I thought I was in wid a chance. Stupid bastard.

"Marleigh, what if he's only been doin' the drug runs because they threatened to hurt ye and he had no choice?" *Like I had no choice wid the Doyles in Ireland.* "How would ye feel about him then? Would ye think of him as a bad person?" *Would ye think* I'm *a bad person if I told ye all the shite I got up tae?*

"I still don't want anything to do with him. He lied to me."

"What if he'd told you from the start what he was doin'?"

"I couldn't be with him."

His heart sank. Not that he'd have a chance with her when David was out of the picture, but hope had burned bright. "So ye're averse tae bein' wid someone who does wrong?"

"Um, technically, morally, I'd have to say yes, wouldn't I?"

"Why?"

"Because if I condone bad things, that makes *me* bad by association."

"I told ye some of what I do, who I am, yet ye seem tae be condonin' that just by me bein' here."

Her forehead creased. "Put like that…"

"What I'm askin' is, David has done wrong, but do ye still love him?"

She shook her head. "I…I love who he used to be, who I thought he was. I married him based on that person. If I'd known he was capable of being dodgy before that, *perhaps* I'd have still married him because I'd have known from the start, but to find out he's not who I thought he was… It's a betrayal, isn't it?"

That was good enough for Ichabod. She knew who *he* was—to a degree—and if he was ever lucky enough to hook up with her, he'd have to tell her everything. About his past, who he'd been, what he'd done.

That would put an end to any of ye daydreamin'. She'd run a mile.

But what if she didn't?

Jaysus Christ, man, she's not interested in ye.

He could pray she might be, though.

"To answer your question properly, truthfully," she said, "the answer is no, I don't love him like I used to. I've been pretending, putting on a front, like so many women do for one reason or another. The shine went off my love for him a long time ago. I stayed because…because I didn't have the courage to end it. And I'm ashamed to say I didn't know what I'd do. I don't work, I have no income. Where would I go? I've been thinking about that a lot since he said he'd be away for Christmas. He didn't seem to care I'd be by myself. Got angry when I pointed that out to him, saying if I wanted to keep living in luxury, I'd shut up and let him get on. He doesn't usually snap at me like that. I rattled around this place by myself, couldn't bear to tell my family he wasn't here. I lied and said we were having a quiet break on our own. It was too embarrassing to admit what was really going on."

"So ye care about what others think, do ye?"

"To an extent, yes."

"Their opinions matter."

"Of *course* they do, they're my family. News of this is going to crush them. And his. God, his poor mother."

He hadn't got his point across enough. "Look, one day ye might wake up and *not* care what people think—I hope ye do, because livin' that way is so much easier. What he's done isn't your fault. When—or if—people find out, it isn't a reflection on ye, and so what if people suspect ye were in on it? Ye know ye weren't, and that's all that counts."

She cringed. "I've been brought up to be respectable."

So was I, and look how that turned out. "Ye can hardly claim tae be that when ye've admitted ye fell out of love wid him yet stayed wid him because of the money."

She winced. "Ouch."

"We've all got a bit of bad in us. Acceptin' that is the way forward." He'd been selfish, saying what he had to her. Letting her see she had maggot-ridden reasons for doing things inside her, too. It was to show her she shouldn't be pious, she should view the broader picture and accept not everyone was perfect. Her or him. If she could see that in herself, she might be more receptive to…

Who was he kidding? A woman like her wouldn't go for a man like him.

"I know I've got bad in me," she said. "My diary is testament to that. The things I've put in there, terrible thoughts, spiteful things…"

"It's natural." He'd planted the seed and would wait for it to grow. "Ye don't want him dead, but ye must have known he might end up that way if ye contacted the twins. Is that one of ye nasty thoughts?"

She nodded. Tears fell. "I'm a horrible person."

"No, ye're hurt, he lied tae ye, and ye're angry and want tae get back at him. The twins might decide he goes missin'. Ye *know* what that means."

"I do."

"If David *wasn't* coerced into gettin' involved wid drugs, are ye prepared tae face the fallout? Tae play the part of the woman whose husband didn't come home? Ye've basically signed his death warrant by gettin' the twins involved if those drugs have reached Cardigan. Ye'll have tae phone the police, say he didn't arrive home as planned. Ye'll have tae pretend ye're worried about him. It's a long time before he can be declared dead. Seven years. Can ye handle that?"

"He should go to prison."

"The time for that has come and gone. George and Greg hold all the cards now. Maybe ye should have thought about what ye were *really* doin' before ye rang them."

"Oh God…"

Her sob wrenched at his heart and, may the Lord help him, he felt sorry for her when, if he'd been dealing with someone else, he wouldn't have. He'd have told her she'd made her bed and had to lie in it.

Could him being involved in this muck the operation up? With the strong feelings he had for her, he had to be careful he didn't allow them to overtake his job and how he performed it. She was a mixed-up woman, to be sure, she had layers she hid beneath a perfect veneer, but Ichabod planned to peel them all away and make her see she was just like him.

Bad but good.

Maybe then she'd see beyond *his* outer layer to the man underneath. Someone who'd give all of himself to her for the rest of his life. Never lie to her.

Feckin' fanciful eejit. It'll never happen.

"If I tell ye a bit about myself, will it make ye feel better? Show ye that people can do the wrong thing but still be someone worth knowin'?"

She nodded, so Ichabod began.

Chapter Two

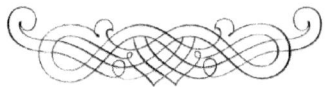

The rolling hills surrounding the expanding village of Caldraich, Northern Ireland, stretched on for miles. Houses were being erected on the outskirts, and at the rate they were popping up, one day it might become a town. Ichabod stood there, disorientated in the gloaming, having been unceremoniously dumped out of a slow-moving vehicle. His hip and knees, so sore from the landing,

might give him some gyp when he walked. He'd ripped the black hessian sack off his head and now stared after a white Transit.

One he recognised.

"Feckin' Doyles. Bastards."

It made sense now, what they'd said, wherever the hell he'd been before this. The bag had been jammed over his face from behind in an alley, and they'd bundled him into the van, someone in there with him, holding his wrists together, a knee on his back. They'd taken him somewhere. Probably an out-of-the-way lock-up, knowing that lot. The place had smelled musty, dirty, a bit of damp teasing his senses, and the bag stank of fish.

"If ye don't do what we say, we'll kill ye granny."

He hadn't recognised the voice, whoever it was must have disguised their own, and it seemed stupid, to have hidden their identity, when he now watched the van shoot off around a bend by a hill, heading towards the burn. Why bother when he'd know damn well who they were from the number plate? They hadn't changed their van since the last time he'd visited Ireland, and besides, he'd seen them getting out of it last night at the pub. He'd clocked the plate out of habit, something required of him in his job for the twins.

"Eejits."

They must have been playing with him, making out they were someone else so it upped the scare factor. He hadn't missed that lot one bit. Their games. Their dark stares. The way they thought they ruled the village. Most people avoided them so they didn't get tangled up in their murky shit. Ichabod was glad he'd got away from them young. Their taunts about his big ears had given him a complex. He'd had them pinned back when he was ten, but the Doyles' nickname for him, Rabbit, had stuck, even all these years later.

Ichabod, Mammy, and Daddy had left Caldraich when he'd been little, moving to Liverpool, then to London. His parents were dead now, they'd had him in their early forties, but he returned to Ireland from time to time to catch up with the family. He wished he hadn't chosen the same week as last year now. The Doyles had filed that information away and pounced on him three days after his arrival.

How long had they been planning this? It freaked him out to think that while he'd been in London, living his life, he'd been discussed here, his name bandied about, plans to use him finalised.

He looked around to get his bearings. The chubby spire of St Mary's poked up from the higgledy-piggledy cluster of buildings to his left, far away, but it was walkable. They'd have dropped him here as an inconvenience to him, or maybe they wanted him to think about the job they'd given him on the trek back. Time to 'mull it over'. Like he had a choice. There was nothing he could do. If he packed his bag and returned to London, they'd make good on their threat. He couldn't live with the guilt if that happened.

He could *speak to his cousin, Rowan, get another perspective, but it would mean dragging him into this mess, and he couldn't do that to him, not when Rowan had to live among them.*

And not now I know it's the Doyles.

Ichabod was on his own in this, and wasn't it better that way? If no one other than the Doyles knew what he'd done, he'd likely get away with it. Like the many feuds in the village, what had actually gone down wouldn't be spoken about. He might be suspected, seeing as he'd be returning to London soon. The Doyles wouldn't be, despite the target being their new enemy, apparently, although they hadn't told Ichabod who it was yet, or why. That would come at some point tomorrow. Biffy Doyle, the eldest, had forced Ichabod to give him his phone number. They'd planned an alibi, all the brothers together in the Fiddler's String, enjoying the weekly cèilidh with the violinist and that whacky old fella who banged the drum. Everyone would be drunk, but they'd remember the Doyles.

What they wouldn't remember was Ichabod. He never went to the Fiddler's on a Friday while here. That was when he visited his granny.

They'd been so clever in choosing him. Granny might not recall whether he'd been there or not at the designated time of the hit, what with her mind going, her short-term memory shot to pieces. Cruel of them, to use her situation to their advantage, but then the Doyles weren't known for their kindness.

"Feck's sake."

Ichabod dropped the black sack on the grass verge, his nostrils full of the fish smell. Why fish? He wouldn't put it past those bastards to have poured tuna water on the sack from a can, wanting him to suffer as much as possible.

He headed in the direction of the village. As predicted, he did mull it over, thinking about the pitfalls, how he'd have to creep into Granny's after he'd done the deed, pretend he'd been there at five o'clock, not seven. Possibly confuse the poor woman. The family were after getting her into a care home, but she wouldn't have it. Said the nurse coming in twice a day was enough for her. Although the nurse never visited in the evenings to put her to bed. The family did that between them after watching telly with her for a bit, and Ichabod took Fridays while he was here so Auntie Niamh didn't have to.

Only, he'd be two hours late.

So he'd do what the Doyles wanted, then. He'd clearly made his mind up. He wouldn't run back to the UK. He'd do what they'd said and hope they didn't ask for more, like another quick job squeezed in before he left. Exactly what they got up to as a family he didn't know, apart from the rumours that they killed people if they were crossed. How they earned their money was a mystery, but they lived together in a big old house with six bedrooms, so whatever it was, it was lucrative.

The walk back would take a while, and by the time he arrived at the choppy burn that bisected the hills from the outskirts of the village, the sky had darkened to full night. He'd misjudged his route, having gone from childhood memory, and had to trudge to the left to reach the tall metal bridge that spanned the black snake of water. The moon's reflection on the surface, marred by the wiggly crests of fast-flowing current, seemed to mirror how he felt. A bit broken, the pieces of him not quite fitting together anymore.

Coming here was supposed to be a break from what he did in London, yet he may as well still be there, considering what he'd been instructed to do.

He climbed the many steel steps and reached the middle of Burn Bridge. He sighed, gave the water a long look, then continued on, down the slope of a hill and over one of the Sullivans' fields. The lights in the village centre drew him, brought out his need to go back to his London life where he knew what was what and didn't have that many surprises unless the twins sprang one on him.

He let the familiarity of the area swallow him up. Funny how he'd remembered this place the first time he'd come back, as if he'd never left. His childhood in Caldraich before Liverpool had stuck in his mind, and nothing much had changed bar a few different shops and extra housing. Mammy and Daddy had brought him here every summer for a good old knees-up with the Ahearn family.

He made it to the village twenty minutes later, the serenity of the hills gone now, replaced by the hustle and bustle of residents out for the night. High Street, packed with those eager to fill their bellies with either food or alcohol, meant several people bumped into him, saying sorry then carrying on as if it had never happened. Weird that, how life moved on after an altercation, be it a quick, accidental knock of an elbow in the ribs or a savage murder. The latter was never forgotten, but it faded, the sun still rose and set.

Plenty had been killed around here, all by the Doyles, except no one could prove it was them. If you upset them, you paid the price. Those alibis of theirs were rock-solid. While Ichabod was a foot soldier for the twins in the East End, and he'd murder for them if they ever asked, he didn't relish killing someone here. Ireland was his roots, it was sacred, and it bit a giant hole in him that it would be forever sullied. When he came back next time, he'd recall everything that had gone on here.

He drew a memory forward, of the Doyles, the bullies of his younger years. How frustrating—and embarrassing—that they scared him somewhat as an adult, all of those little-boy feelings still present. It annoyed him because he worked for the twins, *for feck's sake, he had ninja skills and could take someone down in a second, yet they'd still had the ability to unnerve him. The way they'd bundled him into that van after the snatch, he hadn't had time to fend them off, and his brain hadn't engaged in survival mode, instead letting him down.*

He told himself to up his game in martial arts. Never would this happen to him again.

He'd been glad to move to Liverpool because of those Doyle boys, to the safety of the Liverpudlian kids who'd treated him as one of their own, never taking the piss out of his ears or being nasty. If it wasn't for his family, he'd probably never come here because of Biffy, Alastar, and John.

He left town and made his way to the housing estate where he used to live, where Auntie Niamh still did, and Granny. Uncle Ted and his wife lived over the other side of the village, the type to keep themselves to themselves. Introverts, he supposed they'd be called nowadays, only venturing out to do their stints at Granny's or go to work. Mammy's family didn't live in Caldraich anymore, all of them moving away. Next time Ichabod visited Ireland, he'd make a stop in Bessbrook to see them.

He entered the Fiddler's, two cottages converted into a pub, an old-fashioned place with horse brasses nailed to the mantel over dancing flames. Each family had specific chairs and tables, those who preferred standing a designated spot. Weird, but it worked. Mammy had said it was a tradition from over a century ago, one nobody wanted to disregard.

The people of Caldraich were a strange bunch.

Biffy Doyle stood in front of the fire with his brothers. The lot of them laughed and talked loudly. To anyone watching, Biffy only gave Ichabod a cursory glance, as if he wasn't important. But Ichabod knew better. Biffy's eyes—something about them spoke to him: Keep ye mouth shut, ye eejit prick. Think of ye granny.

Ichabod nodded to him and went up to the bar, hacked off that his body shook when he was more than the little boy he used to be. It wasn't through fear for himself anymore but for Granny. The thought that they'd go through with their threat and hurt her if he disobeyed them had him fuming. He could reach out for help, ask the twins to come here and deal with the Doyles, but that was a big ask, one he wasn't prepared to request. This wasn't like London, where George and Greg could creep in, grab the Doyles, then take them off to beat the shite out of them. Coming here would leave a footprint unless they used fake identities.

"Dia duit, Rabbit. What can I get ye?" Aoife Gallagher, the landlady, asked.

Ichabod said hello back. Aoife smiled her winning smile (dentures), grey strands of hair sticking to her sweaty, ruddy cheeks. She was four-feet-nothing and a jolly sort if you were on her right side, but she also had a temper if you weren't. She often visited Granny during the day when her husband took over the running of the pub. Aoife preferred working the evenings. She said it was more lively and kept her young. She'd never forgotten Ichabod, and whenever he came back, it was as if he'd never left. Many a night he'd sat in here as a child, with Mammy and Daddy during their week's stay, a glass of Coke and a packet of crisps his treat, free of charge from Aoife.

He nodded to the pumps. "A pint of the black stuff."

She glared at him. "Ye mammy, God rest her soul, brought ye up better than that."

"Le do thoil." He'd added the 'please' to stop her from scrutinising him in that knowing way she had, and why he had to say what he'd like to drink he didn't know. She knew what he drank. He'd been in here every evening this week.

She slid a glass beneath the spout and pulled the pump handle to pour. "Are ye on a bender like the last few nights?"

He hadn't planned to drink himself stupid this evening, he'd prefer a clear head for tomorrow, but it'd look weird if he didn't act the maggot. "Am I gettin' predictable?"

"Everyone around here is these days. Not so much in the past, though."

That was a bit mysterious.

She placed his pint of Guinness on the bar, then whipped a card reader from beneath it and held it out.

"Go raibh maith agat." He thought he'd better say thank you before he forgot. God knew she'd ream him a new arsehole otherwise. He took his wallet from his

pocket, removed his debit card, and tapped the reader.
"So ye know everyone's habits, do ye?"

"Of course I feckin' do." *She flashed her dentures again.* "Like I know ye won't be in here tomorrow night for the cèilidh, ye'll be visitin' ye granny instead. That's a shame, because we have a new band comin' in."

"Who's that?" *he asked then sipped his drink.*

"The Silvers. Heard of them over there in England, have ye?"

"No."

"Tsk. Too much London livin' makes ye forget where ye were born. It's goin' tae be like sardines in here."

The more people the merrier for the Doyles—they'd be seen by many. That must have been why they'd chosen tomorrow night for him to do the job. Crafty bastards.

"I'll be sorry tae miss it," *he said.*

"Aye, but maybe ye can switch nights wid someone else so ye can come. Niamh will do it, she's always at ye granny's of a Friday. Sure, she's a good woman. She won't mind."

He thought of Auntie Niamh, how she juggled two jobs and coped with her moody husband, Tadhg. Plus Rowan, their son, still lived at home. "Nah, she *deserves a break. She said she'd be goin' tae the bingo in the community hall."*

"So she did." Aoife glanced along the bar. *"I'd better see to this melter."* She jerked her head at old Cormac. *"Bloody annoying man."*

"Grand." Ichabod left her to it, spotting a free seat at the front by the window.

Although the table was occupied, those sitting around it welcomed him, three farmers from the croft farther down from Burn Bridge. The matriarch wasn't there, and he briefly wondered why not. The Sullivans always came here as a family. Niamh hadn't mentioned any deaths since his last visit, so he was sure the woman must be okay.

Lorcan Sullivan, the eldest and father to the others, Finn and Darragh, patted Ichabod on the back. *"How have ye been, Rabbit?"*

"Ye asked me that last night. And the two before."

"Did I?"

"Yes, Da," Finn said. *"Ye was pished."*

"I'm never pished," Lorcan said on a laugh.

"I think ye were." Ichabod smiled. *"Anyway, I'm grand."*

"Good." Lorcan leaned over to whisper, *"You see them Doyles?"*

Ichabod didn't want to turn and give them the once-over. Biffy might spot it. "Yeah."

"I'm tellin' ye, they're up tae plottin'. Biffy, the sleeven, he's got that look about him, so he has."

Ichabod shrugged. "I wouldn't know what his looks are like. I don't live here anymore tae see them, remember. I dare not stare their way in case they start on my ears again."

"But ye ears are fine now, so they are."

"I know, but it wouldn't stop them."

Lorcan supped his pint. Placed the glass down and stared at the froth. Whispered again, "Word has it they're bein' watched by the garda."

Ichabod's stomach rolled over. He didn't need this. Was that why they'd asked him to do the job, so he'd get the blame? Were they going to set him up? Make sure he got caught? "What for?"

"Drugs."

Ichabod's muscles loosened with relief. The job was nothing to do with drugs as far as he knew. "Ah, I don't know anythin' about those."

Lorcan eyed him. "What were ye doin' out on Burn Bridge earlier?"

Feck. He'd been seen. Maybe Lorcan had spotted him from the farm. Or it was probably when the Sullivans had driven past in their Land Rover to come here. He must have been so inside his head he hadn't heard or seen it. He'd have to be more careful come tomorrow.

"I went for a walk."

"Got troubles in the Big Smoke ye needed tae mull over, have ye?"

"Nah, just needed some exercise."

"Best not tae go on them hills."

"How come?"

"Only, the bridge is where the Doyles have been doin' their drug exchanges of a Thursday. I've seen them up there week on week. I wouldn't want ye tae get the finger pointed at ye as collectin' it for them this week."

"Who's been doin' it?"

"I'm not sure. Never have been able tae make him out. But the Doyles come by in that van of theirs tae pick him and a suitcase or two up. The people who deliver them walk across my bloody field and into the village. They have balaclavas on."

"How can you see it all that clearly?"

"I've got a telescope. Finn bought it for me tae watch the stars."

Ichabod's skin turned cold. That explained why the van had gone in the direction it had earlier. He'd bet they'd picked the drugs up on their way to Caldraich after dumping him.

"Keep a wide berth, son."

"I wouldn't touch the stuff. Wouldn't work for them. Got a good job in London."

"Then don't go out that way again, ye hear me? The garda, they'll nab ye, thinkin' ye're one of them. It's only a matter of time."

"I'm not, never would be."

"Make sure it stays that way."

Lorcan turned to his sons and joined in their conversation about wheat. Ichabod drank his Guinness, crapping his pants. Had the Doyles dropped him off in the hills as an extra warning? Showing him if he didn't do what they'd asked, not only would they kill Granny, they'd whisper in a garda's ear and get him fingered for their drug shit?

With the twins, he was always told exactly why things were being done, why he had to do it in a certain way. With the Doyles, he'd had nothing. It just proved what a bunch of novices they were in comparison.

But they can't be tae bad at what they do because they've never been caught.

To take his mind off the upcoming job, he laughed at something Lorcan said to disguise the fact he was uneasy. What if officers had gone past on that road and had seen him on the bridge? All right, no one else had been on it, so it was obvious he hadn't collected anything, but a garda could be in the Doyles' pocket. They could say they'd seen Ichabod doing a drug deal, just to blame it on him.

Finally, he had the courage to look over at Biffy.

The big man stared back, a smug smile fixed on his ugly face, as though he knew something Ichabod didn't.

As though I've just made a colossal mistake.

Chapter Three

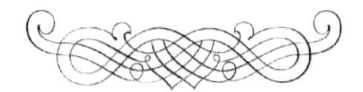

The twins sat with DI Janine Sheldon in Nessa's office in the Noodle and Tiger. Nessa had provided coffees and returned to work, giving them some privacy. Colin, Janine's DS, had been sent off to poke about in some case or other they were working on to get him out of the way. In a message, George had explained to Janine that they needed to speak today, urgently, and no, it couldn't wait until she'd clocked off tonight, and also no, he didn't care if she was seen going into the pub. She'd had the sense to enter via the back door that led to the car park.

"What the fucking hell are you playing at?" Janine hissed from across the other side of the desk. She'd commandeered Nessa's comfy chair over the two hard foldout ones and sat there as if she were a CEO. The one in charge. "This had better be something good. I can't have Colin asking me questions because I've switched my work phone off. What if he tries to contact me? And I've got some poor cow on my hands who was killed on Boxing Day in a domestic violence incident. Her husband's fucked off so he's likely done it, and her kids have been shipped to family they hardly know because there's no one else to look after them. They found their own mother covered in blood, hacked with a knife in her bed. They're four and five, for fuck's sake, their poor little minds will be ruined. So *this*, whatever it is, I don't need."

George ignored her outburst after a kick to the shin from Greg that warned him not to get on his high horse, not today. Not when they needed her. George contemplated whether he'd take heed.

Perhaps for now. But any more of her chatting shit, and he wouldn't hold back.

He *did* feel bad for the dead woman and her kids so asked, "Did the murder happen on Cardigan?" If it had, he'd sort some money towards a funeral.

Janine slumped back. "No, just over the border on the Moon Estate, so you can keep your sticky beak out."

George wasn't going to stand for that, no matter what his brother did or said. "Oi, you're getting on my chuffing tits lately, barking at me. Rein it in, will you? I've said that before and you've ignored me, but I mean it this time. You might have had a shitty past, and I feel for you on that, but this is the present, and I won't keep taking your crappy attitude."

She glared at him. "What are you going to do if I don't behave? Kill me?"

At one time he'd have said yes, but he'd grown fond of the spiky Janine, despite her smug grin. "Don't be stupid. I'd just whisper in your senior's ear that you're bent. Send him that video of you in the warehouse, the one we filmed for insurance. Fuck up your life to get back at you."

"You mean it, don't you."

"Yep. Now tell me what's up. And no lying."

She sighed as if her life was already fucked up. "I'm stressed to the eyeballs like you wouldn't believe."

He noted she hadn't apologised. She was more like him than he cared to admit. Stubborn cow. Maybe that's why she got on his nerves more often than not. He didn't like seeing parts of himself staring back at him. Parts he still had to work on. Despite that, he was getting better at trying to fix his downfalls. That counted for something, didn't it? He wasn't anything like he used to be. Changing yourself was a long process, a winding road, but he'd get there in the end. He just wished Janine would join him on that path.

"But that's nothing new," she added. "Stress is my middle name."

"Work?" he asked.

"No, my private life." She flushed, as if she shouldn't have said that—or wished she hadn't. "Oh, now I've really opened a can of worms. Well done, Janine." She rolled her eyes at herself.

George lurched to the only conclusion he could come to. He thought of the bodyguard they'd assigned to her, the man she'd taken a shine to and lived with now. "Is Cameron treating you okay? If he's gone funny on you, you'd better fucking tell me. It's our fault he's your bodyguard, we picked him, so if we've sent a dodgy bastard your way without knowing it... We had him thoroughly checked, so if he's been hiding a darker side all this time..."

"No, he's fine, he's brilliant. It's something else."

"Like what?"

Janine sighed again, defeated. "Look, I may as well tell you—I wasn't going to, not yet, but it might help you to understand why I'm so tetchy. Or more tetchy than usual. Jesus, Cameron doesn't even know yet, so this feels all kinds of wrong, and I only got it confirmed recently, so it's all new to me. It's scary and confusing."

"Confirmed? Are you being transferred? That's all we fucking need."

"Nothing to do with my job—the one at the station."

What did that mean? "Stop being cryptic and spit it out. You know I don't like riddles, they make me stabby. We won't say jack shit to Cameron, this is between us. Have you realised you prefer being single and don't know how to tell him? Because I'll do it for you if you like."

"What, bull at a gate?" Greg said.

George bristled. "I *can* be tactful sometimes, you know."

Greg laughed. "Pull the other one."

"You know damn well I can. I'll list all the occasions if necessary."

"That won't be hard because you could tick them off on one hand."

Janine slapped the desk. "For fuck's sake, you two, shut up! I'm pregnant." She stared as though those last two words had shocked her.

"Oh, fuck me sideways." George dragged a hand down his face, his mind immediately going to how this would affect them and the running of Cardigan. Selfish of him, but wouldn't that be most people's reaction? "I thought you didn't *want* kids. That's one of the reasons we chose you for the job. No ties."

"I don't—didn't. Shit, I don't *know* what I want, *okay*? I'm still trying to get my head around it. This is a big thing for me. But in case I decide to go through with it, you might want to do your research on another bent copper to replace me while I'm on maternity leave. Or forever."

Forever? Is she taking the fucking piss?

"Right." George bashed his temper down into a little steel box in his mind. She didn't need him bleating on at her about such things as condoms or the pill, but he itched to say it. Give her a lesson in sex education. "Thanks for warning us early enough. Got any recommendations?"

"I've been thinking about it. Look at Bryan Flint. He's the only one who seems remotely suss to me and likely to be turned. He's overly nice at work, and it doesn't sit right. As if he's hiding who he really is."

"Has he got any kids?"

"No. He's single, too."

George glanced at Greg, taking the hint from what his brother *wasn't* saying: *Ask her how she is, you melt.*

George had a word with his temper, his greedy need to keep her on their books, and strangled them. "Are you holding up? Was it a shock?"

"Of *course* it was a fucking shock! Jesus! I'm all over the place. A big part of me wants it, because Luke got right into my heart, and another part doesn't. I'm trying to work out which part is bigger. Once I let Cameron know, he's going to be so happy. It'll be hard to tell him it's not a path I want to go down. He knows I don't want kids but saw how I was over Luke. He's convinced I want a baby now." A choked noise came out of her. "And what if I do, deep down? What if I want shitty nappies and pushchairs and being puked on? What if getting minimal sleep turns out to be right up my alley?"

"Fucking hell," George muttered. "You're tetchy enough on a full night's sleep, so I feel sorry for Cameron when you're up all night. He'll probably need to wear a plastic jockstrap so his balls don't ache when you kick him in the dick."

She fought a smile. The smile won. "Very funny."

But George couldn't deny what she'd said. Luke had got into many people's hearts, not just hers. He'd been born prematurely, dead, and taken to St Matthew's church by the man who'd pushed the baby's mother over, bringing on labour. Janine had worked the case, and clearly, she'd been emotionally involved. For her to even *consider* having a child, well, she must have been affected more than George thought.

Or maybe her biological clock had recently piped up, gassing in her earhole about her regretting it if she didn't take the chance to have a child now.

"Anyway." She brushed the air as if moving her lingering words out of the way. "What do you sodding well want?"

George marvelled at how easily she could switch off her issues and get on with the job at hand. He supposed she'd learned how to do that, like he and Greg had, because their pasts were so traumatic. That was why she fitted in with them. She knew when to cry and when to have that British stiff upper lip. Keep calm and carry on.

He explained what had been going on with David. At the end, he massaged his temples, his head throbbing. "I realise you can't go poking about regarding the drugs, that'll be another department. All I want is for someone to make a little phone call."

"Me, you mean."

"Obviously. We need to know when he's due to touch down at London City Airport, what the flight number is. His wife hasn't got a clue. He doesn't tell her things like that. We're going to nab him as quickly as we can after he lands."

"Drugs." Janine shook her head. "Is that why you're involved? You reckon they've made their way to Cardigan?"

"I don't know for sure, but I aim to find out. If he's working for another leader to bring it in, this is the first we've heard of it. We have to be upfront at leader meetings on shit like that, and no one's said they've got a David Jasper acting as a smuggler."

"I'm not nosing about using a police computer," she said.

"Nope, I want you to pretend to be his mum."

"Oh, for fu—"

"Use your…well, I was going to say charm, but you don't have any. Use your wiles to get the info out of whoever you need to speak to at the airport. Some bird on the help desk. Marleigh doesn't even know where he's gone, so you're going to have to do it with his name alone."

"Why can't she do it?"

"Because we don't want a record of her using her phone or her name being in the equation."

"She could use one of your burners."

"True. But she might fuck up. Say the wrong thing. You know how to keep your wits about you." He gave her a wink. "But that's debatable now. You're likely suffering from baby brain." George laughed.

Greg kicked him again. "Leave it out, bruv. Her hormones are all over the fucking place, so stop winding her up."

George smiled. "Aren't they always?"

Janine glared at him. "D'you know what? You're a fucking arsehole."

He held his hands up. "I know. Good innit?" Going by her face, he'd pushed her too far. "All right, I'll stop rubbing you up the wrong way. Just do this little thing for us and we'll kit the baby's nursery out as a thank-you present."

She bristled. "I can do that myself."

"I know, we pay you enough, but we'd like to help."

Greg butted in. "We'd kit it out anyway, so he's talking bollocks about a thank you. It'd be like our niece and nephew. We'll spoil it rotten."

Janine's smile gave away her feelings—she was chuffed. "What are you going to do with him, this David?"

George shrugged. "Most likely kill him."

"Bloody hell! Is he going in the Thames, or is this something that will land on my doorstep at work?"

"Dunno, I need to speak to Ichabod. He's with Marleigh now, seeing if he can get more out of her than she gave us." He paused. Smiled. Gestured to her belly. "So…congratulations?"

She huffed out a breath of frustration at the subject of her pregnancy being revisited. "I swear to God… I've not long *said* I don't know whether I'm keeping it."

"Let us know when you make up your mind." George sobered. "I'm being serious now. Despite you being a mardy cow most of the time, we wouldn't want you or the baby coming to any harm with you working for us, so the sooner you make a firm decision, the sooner we can approach this Flint fella once we've done all the research on him."

"What, you'd take him on before I go on mat leave?"

"Yep. You've become important to us. We kind of like you. I'll reiterate: we don't want you put in any danger."

Her eyebrows rose. "You *kind of* like me. Right."

George grinned. "Okay, we care about you. Now fuck off, that's all the sentimentality you're getting out of me, unlike my brother who's let the secret out about how *much* we care about you. Twat. Go and do your job."

She rose and walked to the door, turning to look at them. "I like you, too, just so you know, even though you, George, are a total tosser sometimes. And thanks for not coming down on me like a sack of shit about this." She laid a hand over her flat belly. "I've been worrying about leaving you in the lurch. And if I'm honest, I hate the idea of letting someone else take over from me, but I'll have to get over it."

George smiled. "Sounds to me like you've made your mind up."

She blinked. Thought about that. "Hmm, maybe I have."

Chapter Four

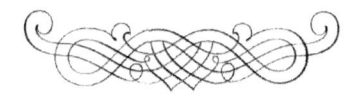

Marleigh had often been baffled about who she was inside sometimes compared to what she showed other people. How she'd forced herself to hide all of her bad thoughts, only putting them in her diary, and even then feeling guilty about them. Did everyone experience that? People couldn't be perfect all the time, she was well aware of that, but her gut instinct, in anger, to phone The Brothers about David... It was a little mean, wasn't it? Going a bit too far, considering she knew they might kill him? Did lying to her, bringing drugs into the country, deserve the fate of death?

"What are ye thinkin'?" Ichabod asked.

"Whether what David's done is worth killing him over."

Although the discovery of the ledger had proved he went away to collect drugs from wherever the hell he went to, she'd still suspected he was having an affair as well, that thought loitering, never fully going away, even though she'd tried to talk herself out of believing that a hundred times. And here she was, thinking it again.

"Personally, I'd want tae cut his cock off."

Marleigh smiled. "I've imagined doing that myself plenty of times, then changed my mind, because while he was attentive to me when home, he *was* different, more so lately. On edge, snippy, pacing, as if the weight of the planet sat on his shoulders. I should be more sympathetic."

After all, it could be like Ichabod had said and David had been forced into doing what he did—

but the lies, they boiled her soul, leaving her suffocating on the condensation.

"I want retribution. Some kind of *sorry*."

And if he *was* seeing someone else, well… Death was more serious than her angrily keying a scratch down the side of his car in temper or slicing up his clothes, things other women would do.

"I have no idea how I'd react if he tells me the truth. I might fly off the handle more than I imagined. I might *want* the twins to kill him."

Obvious things pointed to another woman: text messages that turned his face red; that odd mix of perfume and his aftershave; taking phone calls upstairs, claiming they were for work, yet he'd always just gone into the kitchen before. And that one in the middle of the night six months ago, when he'd come back to bed smelling of alcohol, and in the dim light from the moon shining behind the curtains, she'd caught his smile. More like a grin.

But they could be explained, too. The drug boss could have sent the text, telling him off, then phoned him. And it could be a woman who ran the outfit, and that's why the perfume lingered on his clothes. He could have got good news that night, a bonus, maybe. But an affair didn't quite add up. She'd seen him playing with himself in the shower when she was *right there*, willing to have sex with him, so why was he doing that?

He might be fantasising about the other woman.

Did he pretend he was with *her* when he had sex with Marleigh?

Was she guilty as well, though? Didn't that website say an emotional affair was just as bad as an actual one? That her thinking about Ichabod in ways she shouldn't meant *she* was cheating? She blamed the loneliness. All the attention Ichabod had given her during that stint of surveillance. Even though his eyes had been forward, him looking through those binoculars at Goldie's house, he'd replied to everything she'd said — he'd *listened*. Was *interested* in what she had to say.

Her thoughts had been crazy for too long, ping-ponging all over the place. Marleigh pretending all was well in her world, an outward façade she'd created in order to disguise everything, when beneath it all, demons lingered, whispering, spilling lies they'd fabricated in order to send her mad. But *were* they fabricated? Or did they tell her the truth she'd tried to ignore?

And was she *already* mad to think demons spoke to her?

Having talked some of it through with Ichabod she felt better—he had a way about him that had her feeling as if her emotions were valid, that it was okay to think bad things. She just wanted the truth from David, that was all. She wanted him to look her in the eye and say he was a drug mule who was having sex with someone else. That would mean she wasn't imagining things, and she could rest easy knowing she'd been right. But what if he told a different story? Could she forgive him, even though she'd fallen out of love with him a while ago? It would still hurt, wouldn't it?

As for her admitting she'd stayed with him because of the money and a roof over her head… She'd pushed herself to be brave there. Only her diary had seen such words, and her mind, where they'd swirled and coiled, bringing on guilt, apprehension, anxiety. But now she'd had time to think about it, *David* had been the one to tell her she didn't have to work, he'd said he preferred her to be at home. *He'd* been the one to orchestrate her life. She'd realised, too late, that he was controlling, *not* the fabulous man who'd wanted to coddle her.

That realisation had shrivelled all the love she'd had left for him. That and the drugs, the possible mistress. It was too late now, to go back, to paper over the cracks and pretend, yet again, that everything was okay. She knew more than she wanted to, and nothing could erase it.

They said people reached the point of no return eventually.

Ichabod had told her a bit about his past in Ireland, and far from it shocking her, she'd been drawn to him even more. The danger of him, the menace. The excitement. Yes, he'd told her he'd had to kill someone, but… Was she weird to *like* that? When she supposedly had morals about drugs and numerous other things?

Who the hell am I?

He wasn't as rich as David, could never give her a house like this, the money, the lifestyle, but she was sure he'd always be honest with her, treat her like a princess in the ways that mattered. The Irishman's looks weren't what she'd usually go for, but the chemistry smudged all of his imperfections. He had a presence about him she'd liked from day one. Many a time, when she'd sat with him as he'd spied on Goldie, she'd wondered what it would be like to be with him. To daringly suggest they go to bed. She'd just wanted to be close to the man—and maybe that was all it was. Being left here on her own so often, perhaps she'd craved company, intimacy. Maybe she was getting her attraction to Ichabod confused with something else—she'd been desperate to be wanted. Seen. Needed.

He'd told her he hadn't always been so smartly dressed. That he'd been more than rough around the edges in his skinny jeans, tracksuits, and trainers, his hair unkempt, not having two pennies to rub together. He hadn't put a suit on except for funerals and weddings (and he'd had to borrow them off friends, at that), whereas now he paraded around in them at the casino, had a rail of them in his wardrobe, thanks to the twins. Today, his grey three-piece and white shirt did things to her emotions, and his voice, that accent…

Was she guilty of latching on to him as the next man to take care of her now she'd made up her mind to get rid of David? Was she a user, only out to secure her future? Could she only function if a man provided for her?

She put those thoughts to Ichabod now, cringing inside while waiting for his response. He was going to think she was dreadful, someone he should avoid.

A bitch.

He shook his head. "What people don't understand is that we *all* have thoughts that others would think were nasty. We don't say them out loud because we'd look bad. I read somewhere that ye first thought is ye true self, then the brain takes over and changes it tae somethin' else, somethin' we've been taught is nicer, so we fit in like good little people. I'm not sayin' we should always act on those first thoughts, because I'll tell ye, some of mine have been rotten, but…"

"Like wanting to push someone ahead of me in the supermarket because they're dawdling? Or slap someone just to shut them up, to make them go away? Or raking my nails down someone's face because they annoy me to the degree that I can't stand it?"

Ichabod nodded. "Like I said, we all have them, we just don't say so." He reached out and took her hand. "Wantin' tae secure ye future isn't a bad thing. All right, using David tae get that security doesn't shine a good light on ye, but ye loved him at first, didn't ye?"

"Of course I did."

"And if ye're worrin' about latchin' on tae me as a safety net, feel free tae latch anyway."

Dare she hope he felt the same way about her?

"There has to be something there before I get involved with anyone." Would he pick up on what she meant? That for the first time, despite Ichabod not being able to give her mega riches, she didn't *care*?

The demons whispered again, telling her she *did* care deep down, and tears pricked her eyes. She'd got used to being able to buy whatever she wanted. He couldn't provide that, and she felt like the cow he ought to see her as.

"I sometimes think I'm mad," she said. "I'm alone a lot so only have books or the television, and they're not enough to stop the voices." Oh God, she'd given away her biggest secret.

He didn't let go of her hand, didn't rear back at the mention of the voices. Instead, he seemed to understand, the way he looked at her said so. "A lot of us have voices, too, and again, we just don't say so. Sometimes they're our own, sometimes not. George, he's got the motherload.

Ye're all right, so ye are. Everythin' will work out in the end."

Could she believe that? Could she trust that her daydreams about Ichabod were from a real attraction to him, the chemistry they seemed to share, and not because she needed him to look after her? With him, oddly, she didn't even mind if her family thought him unsuitable. That had to count for something, didn't it? It meant she'd grown out of her hidden shallowness somewhat. Wasn't it better to be with someone who adored you, right down to their core, than be bothered about whether they fitted a certain mould?

Maybe she was just now realising what meeting the right person for her meant. She'd thought that was David, yet she hadn't felt *these* things with him. This need to be close in ways she'd never wanted before, hadn't even thought existed. To have these frank conversations instead of having to squirrel her thoughts and feelings away in case she was laughed at—and knowing Ichabod wouldn't think badly of her for it.

Could she finally be her true self with him?

Would he even want her that way?

He'd never been inappropriate, always polite, so she had nothing to gauge whether he found her attractive. Yes, he held her hand now, but that was more to offer support than anything, and he'd seemed hesitant to reach out, as though he thought she'd bite his head off for touching her.

But he told me to latch on.

"I like you," she blurted.

He smiled. "That's good tae know. Even though I told ye some of what I did in Ireland?"

"Even then."

"I haven't told ye the half of it."

She took a deep breath. "But you can, and I'll listen. I'll try not to judge." She paused. "I'm worried I'm going to cling to you now, for you to save me so I don't have to start again on my own. It's important to me that I don't fall into the same trap as I did with David—I can see now that I used him."

"What are ye sayin'? That ye *like* me, like me?"

Her cheeks grew hot. "Yes?"

"Ah, for the love of God, ye must be messin' wid me."

"Don't you feel it? There's something there, isn't there? Please tell me I'm not imagining it."

"It's there. Look, I have tae tell ye what's goin' on wid me. It's about another job I'm on. For the twins. There's this woman…"

"Oh."

"No, not like that. She's been after me takin' her on dates, and I've turned her down every time because I can't get ye out of my head, but George and Greg need me tae make out I'm interested in her so I can get information."

Dread and shock combined in her stomach. "Are you doing the same to me?"

"Feck no, ye've been on my mind ever since I met ye, but her? She could be sellin' drugs on behalf of her dead sister, without permission, and I need tae find out if she is. I've told ye about it because I want tae be honest—I'll be seen out and about with her Up West, so I don't want ye thinkin' anythin' of it, especially with how ye've thought David was havin' an affair. Not that me and ye are a couple, I just…" He shook his head. "I don't know what we are, but I've told ye now, so…"

She laid her hand on his arm. "I don't know what we are either. I need to make sure I'm not using you for the wrong reasons. Maybe I should be by myself for a while, work out who I am, make sure I don't hurt you."

"It'd look suss if anythin' happened between us at the minute anyway. Wid David bein' missin', which is what I'm sure will happen." He nodded to himself. "Get ye head straight. Take some time. I can wait."

That was different. David had pushed for their marriage, love-bombed her—wasn't that what it was called these days? She'd been so swept up in feeling adored and living a life of luxury that she hadn't stopped to inspect what was really going on. It was only now, with hindsight, and learning that David wasn't this perfect specimen, that she could look back and see where she'd gone wrong.

Yes, learning who she was first, it was a good idea.

"He has life insurance. I won't get that for seven years either. There are savings in a joint account, but would I even be allowed access to it if he's missing? God, I can't believe I just said that out loud."

"Put it down tae bein' practical. Ye've got a lot tae digest, knowin' ye husband will likely be killed. Maybe I can persuade The Brothers tae leave his body somewhere instead of feedin' it tae the fishes." He scratched the side of his head. "But their copper, she's gettin' a bit worried about them keep doin' that. The other pigs are suspicious there's a vigilante goin' around killin' people." He sighed. "Leave it wid me."

"Will I get the chance to speak to David before...before they...?"

"Yes, but ye'll have tae keep it quiet, never tell anyone. Otherwise, the twins will...well, they won't be happy."

A frisson of fear went through her. She knew what George and Greg were like. Everyone understood that Estate leaders didn't suffer fools gladly and protected their patches, killing people if necessary. She just hadn't contemplated that they might kill her. She'd have to keep the secret forever. Not even put it in her diary. Lie to everyone she knew about David dying. Pretending, pretending, pretending.

"I won't tell a soul," she said.

Ichabod nodded. "Ye'd better not, else what would I do if they put ye six feet under, eh?" He paused. Thought. "And how will ye feel when it's me who'll be slicin' David's throat? Because it will be."

He'd said it so calmly, no menace involved. She needed to know more about this man before she committed herself to him. She had to know everything, all the ugly, wicked things, and he needed to know hers.

If they were going to start a life together, there would be no lies this time.

"Tell me about the actual murder in Ireland," she said. "All of it."

Chapter Five

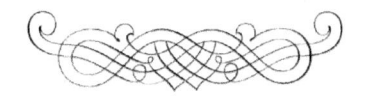

Out of breath because he'd walked all the way here in the cold, Ichabod hid behind a partially open door in the darkness. Butter-yellow light came through the crack, spilling a shaft onto the knobbly concrete of the area outside the barn-like structure. Biffy's weird look in the pub had made sense the minute Ichabod had been told, in a message, who the target was. Or targets. There were four of them. He'd only agreed to the one

murder when he'd been snatched, but it wasn't like he could refuse to kill the others, was it.

Like he'd thought, he had *made a colossal mistake. He'd sat with the Sullivans in the pub, and they were who he'd been sent to murder. Lorcan. Darragh and Finn, lads he'd been to school with. And their mother, the kind and lovely Caoimhe who'd packed up a picnic basket whenever he'd played with her boys as a child, sending them off into the hills to get out of her hair. Suspicion may fall on him now. People would have seen him at their table, especially Aoife, who was a seriously nosy beak. He'd be questioned by the garda because he'd sunk a few pints with them. Someone would pass on that snippet, he wouldn't get away with not being interviewed.*

He prayed Granny wouldn't have a lucid moment if she was asked what time he'd arrived at her house later this evening. She had those moments, not often, but it would be sod's law for her to inadvertently drop him in the shite. The luck of the Irish definitely hadn't been with him on this visit.

"The garda will be there to catch them next Thursday," Lorcan said, his voice floating outside.

"But it's open space!" Finn sounded exasperated — or on the edge of panic. "They'll be seen on the bridge.

The Doyles won't go anywhere near it if they see someone there who shouldn't be."

"I didn't ask our contact for the ins and outs," Lorcan said. "I expect they'll take photos of the handover from a van or something. Long-range camera? I don't know. They could park behind a hedge. I'm just tellin' ye what's goin' on next week so ye keep away from the area until it's all over. We don't want tae be drawn in. We can't have the Doyles suspectin' it was me who grassed on them."

Feck... They've already found out, man. They know.

"They'll probably know ye spotted what was goin' on anyway because the farm's so close by," Darragh muttered. "I told ye not tae risk it, telling on them. I've heard ye whisperin' tae people about it, even Rabbit last night. Then those people will whisper tae others, and it won't be long before someone tells them. There are snakes out there who pretend not tae like the Doyles when really they do."

"Rabbit's grand, he won't say anythin'," Lorcan said.

Ichabod felt so bad he had the urge to go in there and tell them what was going on. Lorcan had been so good to him, a steady influence, a kind and gentle man, but there was Granny to think of, and she came first.

"And it's not just ye they'll go for but us, too," Darragh said. *"Mammy can't defend herself if they come for us. She's a sittin' duck for those heathens."*

"I should have sent her to Auntie Bridget in Kilkenny," Lorcan said. *"Why didn't I do that? Feckin' hell."*

"That's what I want tae know," Finn snapped. *"She's vulnerable now. She can't run away if they break in tae kill us in the night. And ye know that's what they'll do. They're sneaky bastards."*

"I'm sorry, son. Jaysus Christ, I'm so sorry. I've fecked up, so I have."

Ichabod shook his head. How many other people had Lorcan told about the drug swap on the bridge apart from his 'contact'? And who was that? Someone in the garda, for sure. The Doyles had definitely found out it was him who'd grassed, otherwise Ichabod wouldn't be here.

"We should head down to the cèilidh," Darragh said. *"Show our faces so Aoife doesn't get offended, seeing as she's got a new band in. Mammy will have finished her makeup by now."*

Ichabod stiffened. Held the gun tight. Even though it had a silencer on it, it would still be audible. The farm was well away from the village, so that cut out a lot of potential ears, but it might not stop Caoimhe from hearing it. Once he let the bullets fly, he only had a certain amount of time to get to her in the farmhouse. Before she phoned the garda.

"Let me finish this whisky," Lorcan said.

"Maybe we should go away for a couple of weeks, until this is all over," Darragh said. "Once they're caught, we'll be safe."

"Who will mind the farm?" Finn asked. "Jaysus, ye're not thinkin' straight."

Wishing the Sullivans had gone away so he didn't have to do this, wishing he could tell them to pack their bags and feck off right now so he could tell the Doyles no one had been at home, Ichabod moved to the hinges and peered through the gap. A thin slice of what amounted to an office met his perusal, Lorcan sitting behind a desk piled with papers, an old-fashioned, big-backed monitor amongst them, the casing yellowed with age. Finn stood behind him, leaning on the wall beside a dog-eared poster with various planting and harvesting times on it.

Where was Darragh? To the left or right?

Ichabod raised the gun and positioned the business end at the gap, level with Finn's forehead. He squinted to make sure he'd hit the mark, hesitating on cocking the trigger. Shit, he'd played with these men as a kid, he remembered paddling in the burn, having a picnic in between pretending to be soldiers. At no point, ever, had he thought he'd have to kill them to save his granny.

He hardened his heart, his mind, and pulled the trigger.

Resighted on Lorcan. Pulled the trigger.

Darragh popped into view, heedless of where the bullets had come from, to tend to his brother and father. "Jaysus feckin' Christ! Oh, Da. Oh feck, not my da!" He turned. Stared right at the gap, tears streaking down his cheeks. "You feckin' bastard! Come in here and look me in the eye and shoot me, Doyle. I know it's ye, a coward who can't step in and execute us, he has tae hide. Answer me, Biffy!"

Ichabod sighted again.

I'm so feckin' sorry.

He let another bullet fly free. Briefly took in the carnage, the blood, the spatter on the poster, the wall. Finn had dropped to the floor, his forehead sporting a hole, his face poking out from the side of the desk. Lorcan slumped over it, a Pisa tower of papers threatening to tumble. And Darragh, on the floor, too, in the foetal position. The stark view of the back of his head showed most of it was missing, half a brain nestled in his skull, strands of his hair lapping up the blood.

With no time to regret his actions, to have changed it so he'd told the Sullivans why he'd been sent, telling them to go away, tonight, and hide until the garda had apprehended the Doyles, Ichabod ran towards the farmhouse, keeping to the edges of the outbuildings until he had to pelt across to where the family parked their cars and tractor. He ducked behind their Land Rover to assess the situation—no headlights on the main road—so he rushed to the front door and pushed it open, the leather of his gloves squeaking.

"Is that you, Lorcan?" Caoimhe called.

Ichabod stood stock-still in the hallway. Just breathed for a moment. Closed the door. It sounded as though she was upstairs. He didn't answer, obviously, but made his way up, frowning at the stairlift seat attached to a metal rail on the wall. Who needed that? Caoimhe? She'd been fine when he'd visited Ireland last year. Had she become poorly in the meantime?

He paused on the landing. All the doors stood open, revealing a bathroom and bedrooms, and Caoimhe sat in a wheelchair in the master, her back to him, her reflection staring at him from a lit-with-bulbs mirror on a vanity table, like famous people used. Her wide eyes and open mouth showed him he'd startled her good and proper, but then she seemed to get a hold of herself, her poker face settling over her features.

She wouldn't know who he was, Biffy had handed him a balaclava earlier, but he still felt as if she could see straight through the wool to the shame burning his cheeks. But she couldn't. What she would *be able to see was the sorrow in his eyes because* he *saw it as he glanced at himself in her mirror, his position in the doorway appearing ominous. Feck, he looked menacing, all in black, some mad bastard who'd come to kill her.*

"Ye're not Biffy," she said, her bottom lip trembling. "Ye're not big enough. So ye must be Alastar or John. I said ye'd come for us, I said ye'd know, but Lorcan said it was all in hand. How did ye find out? Did ye pay the garda tae spill the beans?" She closed her eyes. "Get on wid it, then. Do what ye came tae do and get yeself down tae the cèilidh before it's tae late. I wouldn't want ye mammy tae go through all the shite she will if ye get caught. Ye need an alibi tae save her from tears."

Ichabod recalled the Sullivan woman had always got along with Mrs Doyle, best friends. Erin, her name was. This was wrong, the Doyle brothers not caring whether their mammy was heartbroken over losing Caoimhe. But Ichabod's *family would be if Granny was murdered by them, so there was no contest.*

76

He pulled the trigger. Forced himself to watch her face explode as a penance, fuel for his future nightmares, blood and brain and God knew what hitting the mirror. Her forehead smacked onto the vanity top, bottles of perfume skittering, a couple hitting the floor. A blusher brush toppled off to roll across the beige carpet and came to rest at the edge of a pink fluffy rug.

When the garda arrived, they'd need a strong stomach to view this.

Ichabod hated himself. He'd killed a defenceless woman in a wheelchair.

He was going to Hell.

From the corner of his eye, he caught sight of a light outside—feck, he hadn't factored in the open curtains, thinking he'd be safe here in the doorway. Was it someone with a torch on their way here? No, a set of headlights pierced the darkness on the main road. He backed onto the landing so by the time the car moved along, he wouldn't be seen in the rearview. He waited for several heartbeats, then peered around the jamb.

No taillights.

He left the farmhouse, scouting the road, the red lights on the back of the car pinpricks now, his outfit too dark for anyone to see. He left the gun behind one of the huge tyres on a tractor, like he'd been told—he hadn't questioned it, didn't want to know what they'd do with it next, but he still worried they were going to plant it somewhere that would send suspicion his way. Better that he got caught and took the rap than Granny be dead, though. He'd give up his freedom for her any day of the week.

He kept his eyes peeled and walked into the night, back the way he'd come. He wouldn't go over the bridge but enter Caldraich via the track off the main road, into an alley in town that led to Folly Courtyard, a fountain in the middle, a place people sat to find a bit of peace.

No cameras.

He'd take a minute, compose himself. Stuff the gloves and balaclava in his pocket until he could get rid of them in a safe place. Go to Granny's.

And hope for the best.

Granny sat in her red wingback chair in the living room. It was a recliner type that also moved upwards then forward to help her stand. Her legs regularly seized up on her, so Niamh had said. She fumbled with the button, waited for her seat to rise, then stood, shuffling towards him.

"So who do we have here, then?" she asked.

She hadn't got to the stage where she didn't know who people were, thank God. Her cheeky smile said she was joking about not knowing him. Ichabod had visited her before this evening anyway, near enough as soon as he'd arrived in Caldraich, so she knew he was back in Ireland.

One day, she wouldn't be joking. She'd have no clue who he was.

He bit his tongue to stop tears from forming.

"I don't know, maybe I'm a robber," he said and laughed.

"I've got nothin' for ye tae take, lad. Only what Niamh brought round for dinner, oh, I don't know when it was. Yesterday?"

"It would have been this afternoon. She said she was comin' tae drop off ye washin'. Anyway, I got here at five, remember?" He hated lying to her, muddling her more than she was already, but he'd killed to save her life, so a little fib wasn't so bad.

He prayed she didn't look at the clock and see what time it was now. He worried again that for just one moment, she might recall, if asked later down the line, that it was seven o'clock, not five, that he hadn't *got here earlier.*

She tutted. "So why the devil isn't my dinner done? What have ye been doin'?"

"I was puttin' your washin' away." He'd just this minute done it hastily.

"For two hours?"

"Well, I tidied the kitchen as well. You were tae busy watchin' telly. Shall we ditch dinner here and go to the cèilidh, eat in the Fiddler's? They've a new band on tonight, and the special is meat and tattie pie." The perfect alibi, along with saying he'd been at Granny's for two hours prior to that. So many people would see him, and he could feign shock if the garda came in and announced the Sullivans were dead. And they **would** *come. They'd want to know whether the Doyles were in the pub.*

"But I'm not dressed for it," she said.

"No one's goin' tae be lookin' at ye clothes." He collected her foldable wheelchair from the cramped hallway, wincing at the flash of memory—Caoimhe in hers at the vanity table. He took it into the living room. "I'll just get ye shoes and coat." He left then returned and helped her into the thick jacket, then eased her into the chair and slipped her brogues on.

"I haven't been to a cèilidh for a long time," she said, beaming up at him.

He got lost in her smile, her sparkling blue eyes, the wrinkles on her soft face. He'd done the right thing, taking four lives to save hers. The heartache of grief would belong to others now, not the Ahearns, but regret hung heavy.

"Then it's about time ye did."

He ensured the fireguard was in place in front of the flames in the grate then grabbed a red scarf from a hook in the hallway to break up his black outfit — if he'd been seen on his way back from the farm, people wouldn't recall a scarf because he hadn't worn one then. He wheeled her out of the house, down the front ramp Uncle Ted had built out of wood, and onto the street.

The Fiddler's was only a street away, so the music reached him, muted but jolly, lots of voices singing. At the pub, he pushed her inside, and Aoife had been right. It was like sardines in here, but people saw Granny's chair and moved aside, a path created for her. Ichabod glanced over at the Sullivans' usual table, hiding a grimace that the seats remained empty despite customers needing a seat. Folks had manners in Caldraich, and you didn't sit in someone else's place unless they'd told Aoife they weren't coming.

Squished together in the left corner on a small dais, the Silvers played their music, a young woman with long hair the colour of the Sullivans' wheat, two men behind her, one on the violin, another blowing a flute. She sang in Gaelic, something Ichabod chose to forget while living in London but remembered when he was on home soil. Mammy and Daddy had taught it to him.

Aoife spotted them and waved Ichabod over to a table closest to the end of the bar, one of several reserved for the elderly. He parked Granny there and ordered her favourite, gin and tonic, plus dinner for them both, her face alight with the wonder of being out of that lonely house and back with the locals. Niamh brought her here on a Monday evening for the quiz, saying Granny needed a quieter life now, but Ichabod didn't agree. This was the first time he'd seen her smile like this since Grandpa had died.

He sat, handing her drink over, and she sipped with her thinned-by-age lips, her gaze all over the place, soaking it all in, and maybe she was recalling times past, when she'd been younger and full of life, her mind sharp as a tack. Did she have regrets? Did she wish she'd let loose more often? Lived a fuller life? Then her attention settled on the Silvers, and she tapped her hand on her knee to the beat. Ichabod drank some of his Guinness, glancing around casually, keeping his face straight when his sights landed on Biffy. Ichabod gave a nod, one that could be classed as a greeting, not confirmation that the job had been done, and he received a nod in return. There was no scowl that Biffy was annoyed Ichabod had shown his face here, so maybe they weren't after setting him up.

The balaclava and gloves seemed to burn a hole in Ichabod's pocket at the same time the flush of shame burned his cheeks.

Feck it.

Chapter Six

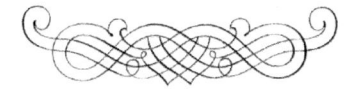

Janine loved the twins—there, she admitted it, all right?—but by God, George had the irritating ability to piss her off one minute and get her smiling the next. Emotional swings and roundabouts. She should be used to him winding her up on purpose now, he likely got a kick out of it, the complex weirdo, but that conversation they'd just had in the Noodle… She'd been more het up than usual and at one point wanted to scream and tell him to go and fuck himself as she wasn't in the mood to deal with him—ever again.

Instead, she'd confessed, surprising herself. Not only because she'd done that, revealing the soft underbelly she preferred to keep hidden, but because of the relief attached in letting those two words come out. I'm pregnant. Christ, such a short sentence yet so heavy.

She got more comfy in the car and thought about a nursery and all the things a baby needed. She could afford the lot, but she'd never seen herself as the type to wander around a shop admiring cots and changing tables or feeling the softness of baby clothes. She couldn't imagine having a big belly, how cumbersome it would be, and she certainly couldn't get her head around someone moving about inside her. A colleague had recently had a child, and she'd shown people how her stomach had changed shape with a hand or foot poking at her.

That kind of thing gave Janine the creeps.

But would she feel the same when it was hers?

Her baby was going to be loved by The Brothers, and wasn't it weird to be fine about it? That George, a fucking maniac, who craved the hot splash of blood on his face and wielding a cricket stump, of all things, would hold her child in his big arms and make sure it was set for life? Maybe to the outsider that would appear horrific, *and* to her once upon a time, but since she'd got to know them, she'd learned they were kind underneath it all and only wanted the best for her. That would extend to her offspring, no question. They were called The Brothers for obvious reasons, yet they were like normal brothers to so many. Janine, Debbie especially, Ichabod, Moon, and all the people they'd helped along the way, one big extended family.

There had been times she'd wished she'd never got involved with them. Extra money and a prestige of sorts at being selected by them aside, her job with those two wreaked havoc with her nerves. If she was going to keep this child, she didn't want her anxious feelings transferring to it while it grew in her womb.

It was best to hand over the reins as soon as possible.

Heat stung her eyes, and she slapped the steering wheel, a lump in her throat. She'd learned to be in control of her life, to monitor all aspects of it since she'd been held in that basement flat against her will, where she'd had no control at all, and at times, no hope of ever getting out. She'd squashed that, though, determined to free herself. To right the wrongs done to her, not just in the flat but regarding her pisshead mother and absent father. To become a police officer to help those in the same situation. The tears that burned annoyed her, because they'd come unbidden, without her say-so.

She'd been so emotional lately, more angry than tearful—or if she could bring herself to be completely honest, fear was the predominant factor, of the unknown. Allowing herself to relinquish her tight hold on everything and just…just go with the flow. Enjoy every moment of her newfound happiness with Cameron. Embrace a baby. Play happy families, something she'd never known, because bloody hell, her childhood had been a strange one, what with Mum the way she was.

When Janine had stared at the pregnancy test stick, a cold sweep of fear had gone through her. What if she was like Mum, unable to look after a child properly? To even want to? What if she brought a baby into the world and ruined it? What if it ruined her? How could someone with such closed-off emotions even begin to share more of herself with another human? She was managing all right with Cameron, but could her heart expand to a third person who would be so ingrained in her life?

"But," a devil whispered, "what if, *because* of your mother, you become the best one around? You fix her mistakes by never acting like her?"

It could work, couldn't it?

She hadn't been lying to the twins when she'd said Cameron would be happy. He'd playfully ribbed her about her attachment to Luke, how she'd changed since working that case. How she might well want a baby of her own—maybe letting her know, in his own way, that he'd be up for it if she did. She hadn't wanted to admit that maternal feelings had swelled inside her, but they had, and now… Now she had a decision to make, but she had a feeling she'd already made it, despite there being more cons than pros.

Their relationship had come on in leaps and bounds, and for her to trust a man after what she'd been through, it just showed how lovely and gentle he was outside of his menacing Cardigan role, one she'd never seen, but he'd told her what he usually got up to. All right, they hadn't been seeing each other that long, but something inside her said they'd be okay. They'd last. God knew how he accepted her spikiness, but he understood why she was like it, and that was half the battle. It didn't mean he should put up with it, though. And she should be more careful around him, treat him with the respect he deserved instead of barking at him from time to time.

She had so much to learn, but her therapist was holding her hand these days.

More tears, and she let them fall this time.

If these hormones were bad now, what would they be like farther along? What if she suffered from post-natal depression and ended up pushing Cameron away? What is she hurt him? Fucking hell, this was why she'd always vowed to stay single until he'd come along. She'd only had to worry about her own feelings, and now…

"Bollocks. Fucking shitting bollocks."

She glanced in her rearview. There Cameron sat, as usual, in his car, paid by the twins to look out for her. The team assigned to The Network case had let her know this morning that they'd almost rounded everyone up. Minions, as they were called. Many had squealed to save their own skins, and only three men were in the wind now, likely living under assumed names, hopefully abroad, well away from her, the copper who'd worked tirelessly to bring the outfit down.

Soon, Cameron might not have to follow her around anymore. He'd be given other jobs to do, likely walking into danger. Danger that might turn fatal and her baby would end up without a father. At least with this assignment she knew he was safe. Knew where he was. Didn't have to worry. But what if George and Greg sent him into a lion's den and he didn't come back out?

What if she lost him?

What if, because he wouldn't be there to protect her, *he* lost *her*?

This was what happened when you opened up to someone and gave them a piece of your heart. It caused problems. It had been such a big thing, letting him in, and she couldn't imagine what it would be like without him now.

The tears burned hotter, and she dashed them away. Took a deep breath.

"Get a fucking grip, you silly cow."

She grabbed her burner phone. Looked up the number for London City Airport and prepared herself to pretend to be some bloke's mother.

But you're someone else's mother, not his…

She swallowed tightly. She *was* someone else's mother.

That hit her with a wallop all over again.

Fuck.

She rang the number and, after being passed around several times, reached the relevant person who could help. Instead of becoming a mum to David Jasper, she threw caution to the wind and used her real name and work title, sod it. So long as she didn't log this conversation at the station, it was unlikely anyone else would know it had taken place.

She got the information she needed and messaged the twins.

JANINE: FLIGHT SCHEDULED TO LAND FROM BRAZIL TOMORROW MORNING AT 10:15.

GG: CHEERS. WHAT COLOUR PAINT DO YOU WANT FOR THE NURSERY?

JANINE: FUCK. OFF.

GG: [LAUGHING EMOJI]

George, has to be. He's such a twat.

But she smiled.

"See? Arsey one minute, laughing the next." She switched the engine on and left the car park, Cameron close behind. She'd tell him tonight.

Jump in with both feet and hope for the best. Welcome this twist her life had taken.

Becoming a new person all over again.

Chapter Seven

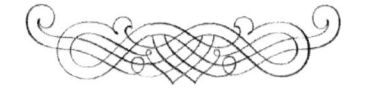

Ichabod had been summoned. He'd left Marleigh's house and drove towards Cardigan. News had come via a message that David would be landing tomorrow morning. What Ichabod's role was now he wasn't sure. He could be assigned to Marleigh while the twins collected her husband or he could be involved in picking him up.

He knew which one he'd choose if given the choice. Marleigh all day long.

But hadn't George mentioned something about using her at the airport to lure David to where he needed to be in order for them to nab him?

Ichabod had been nervous about telling her some of his past. The murder. She hadn't been able to hide her shock at various points, especially the bit about shooting Caoimhe, but he'd seen the gleam of excitement in her eyes. Did she view him as some dangerous gangster? Was that a thing some women got off on? Did he want to be with someone who only wanted to be with him because of what he'd done—and did—instead of who he really was? Was she even interested in the Ichabod beneath the layers and layers of shite he'd draped over his true self to hide the rancid parts?

Time would tell.

To say he'd been shocked at what she'd said—hinting she'd like to see where a relationship with him would lead—was an understatement. All this time he'd been mooning over her, wanting her, wishing things could be different, and now they were, he couldn't quite believe it.

What was it he'd told himself in Ireland? That he wouldn't be like Rowan and let a woman send him daft? He'd failed on that one hundred percent. Marleigh ruled his softer emotions and gave him hope for a beautiful future.

Feckin' hell.

She'd recognised her need to have a man in her life so she didn't have to worry about coping alone. She'd given him respect there, at least, prepared to live by herself until she knew whether she cared for him in a proper way rather than what he could do for her. He'd take her whatever way he could, whether she was using him or not, that's how much she'd got under his skin. The connection they shared, the chemistry, would see them through, he was sure of it.

His mind wandered back to Ireland and the feud between the Ahearns and the Clancys. Now he finally knew the truth of the matter, Rowan telling him all about it, he became unsettled by the parallels. He was prepared to take Marleigh on no matter what, and certain Irish women had done the same with their men, their lives imploding.

He should learn from their mistakes.

Yet the tug towards Marleigh refused to stop tugging. Wasn't it better to have loved and lost than to have never loved at all? Wasn't that the saying?

Jaysus feckin' Christ. Ye're resortin' tae bloody adages now.

He arrived at Cardigan and pulled in down the side of The Angel. Round the back, he tapped on the door to the massage parlour. Amaryllis, a former sex worker now receptionist, opened up.

"All right, Ichabod? They're expecting you."

"I'm fine, so I am. And you?" He stepped inside.

Amaryllis secured the lock. "All good. They're in Debbie's old room."

Ichabod walked over there and knocked on the door.

George swung it wide and grinned. "Have you got past first base with Marleigh yet?"

Ichabod's face grew hot. "Feck off." He went inside and sat by Greg on the sofa.

"Just messing." George shut the door. "But did you?"

"Pack it in," Greg said. "Leave the poor man alone."

George laughed and sat opposite. "So how did it go?"

Ichabod related what he'd found out, not mentioning the private words between them, nor did he pass on about Marleigh falling out of love with David—that might be construed as her wanting to get her own back on her husband, making up a story about him being involved in drugs. He did, however, explain that she thought he might be having an affair, despite finding the ledger and all it contained which could be the sole reason for him going away.

George nodded. "It's the same version she gave us, so that's settled my worries a bit."

Instantly, Ichabod's hackles rose. What was he saying, that Marleigh wasn't to be trusted? *Feck, I need tae watch myself. Maybe I shouldn't be on this job, jumpin' tae her defence.* "What do ye mean?"

"Come on, you know we have to be careful, think about the pitfalls and whether we're being played."

"But why would she be playin' us by shoppin' her husband?"

George scratched his head. "At first she thought he was having an affair, remember? I've got our private dick on that to see if it's got legs. But she might be using us to get back at him."

Ichabod sighed. "I just thought the same."

"So our wavelengths match. You're not completely dazzled by her, still know the job comes first. *Don't* you?"

"Yes."

"Good. The last thing we need is you losing focus. Anyway... You said you contemplated him having a family abroad. A woman and kids. That could well be true. Look at what Belladonna went through with that Mack twat. She didn't have a clue he had another life."

Ichabod's ire ignited. "If he's done that tae her, I'll kill him."

Greg snorted and elbowed him in the side. "I thought you were going to do that anyway. What was it you said? You'd slit his feckin' throat?" The Irish accent on the last line was abysmal.

Ichabod glowered. "Yeah, well, I'll extra kill him."

George barked laughter. "*Extra* kill him?"

Ichabod formed a double fist. "Pack it in, ye know what I mean."

"Okay, serious heads on now." George's face changed from a smile to a hard-as-granite frown.

"We need to discuss what's what, then you can go back to Marleigh and explain, in your persuasive way, that she'll be going to the airport." He paused. "After that, you've got that date with Katy Marlborough."

"Jaysus."

"I know, two jobs on the go isn't ideal, but that's the way it is. Anyway, you might be able to get the information out of Katy quickly. If she's selling drugs in Josephine's place, we can sort her tonight so we can fully concentrate on David tomorrow."

Ichabod settled down to hear the order of play, dreading seeing Katy.

Somehow, it felt like he'd be cheating on Marleigh.

Back at Marleigh's house, cups of tea on the island in the kitchen, Ichabod sat on a bar stool and told himself to just get on with it. Marleigh had said earlier that if they were going to give a relationship a try, she didn't want any lies. They had to spill their truths—the ugliness, the terrible thoughts, the awful deeds, all of it—before they could even think about moving forward.

Now, he had to tell her the blunt truth about which role she'd play in this job. He had to focus on working for the twins, not his connection to her. If he could get through this without letting his feelings for her cloud his judgment, George and Greg would know he could handle anything they threw at him. He owed them so much that it was important for him to prove his worth.

"This may make ye feel like I did when the Doyles approached me. Like ye don't have a choice. I'm sorry tae say, ye don't. The twins have come up wid a plan, and ye're a big part of it. If ye want David caught, ye're goin' tae have tae go through wid it."

She nodded, her expression relating how pensive she was. "What is it?"

"Ye'll meet him at the airport. At his car. He'll have parked it in the long-stay. George and Greg have a couple of men goin' there now tae get its exact location. Ye'll say ye got a taxi there, that ye wanted tae surprise him because ye missed him so much over Christmas. What luggage did he have when he left here?"

"A suitcase, one of those small hardshell ones that can go in the overhead compartment. Silver."

"So if he waltzes along wid another one, a bigger one, then that'll be suss. Ye'll be wearin' a wire, and the twins will be listenin'. They'll be nearby on a main road, probably in disguise, but they don't anticipate David getting lairy wid ye — ye've said he's been snippy but not that he hits ye or anythin'. If he does and ye've kept it from me, I need tae know now."

"No, he wouldn't do that."

"Okay, on the journey home, they want ye tae question him about the second suitcase, if there is one. If he's plannin' tae drop it off before seein' ye, he's goin' tae be antsy that ye're there and he can't. The goal is tae get him home as quickly as possible. George and Greg will follow ye in their taxi all the way."

"Where will you be?"

"After I've dropped ye off at the airport, I'll go back tae your house and wait. If all goes tae plan, it should be simple. Get as much information out of him as ye can, all right?"

"What do I do if he insists he has to stop somewhere first? What if he drives the drugs to whoever he's trafficking them for? What if they hurt me because he's broken a rule by taking me there?"

That was something Ichabod had worried about, too, until he'd been informed of what was going to happen. "Other Cardigan men will be involved. They'll also be following. There's no plan for ye tae be in any danger at any point."

"Right." She straightened her shoulders. "I'll do it. I have to anyway, so…"

He sighed. "Yeah, ye have tae."

She smiled. Nodded to his tea. "Drink that. I'll make us a sandwich while you tell me some more about Ireland to take my mind off everything."

He took a deep breath and thrust himself into the past.

Chapter Eight

As if by some form of telepathic communication from the garda who'd just pushed their way in, a cliché TV show playing out in real life, the Silvers stopped abruptly. Each band member appeared confused by the sudden change in the air; maybe they'd never played in a place like Caldraich where there were unspoken rules that only the villagers knew. It was the silence that must have prompted them to cease mid-

song, each resident more attuned to changes and what they could mean.

Ichabod's guts rolled. Customers snapped their mouths shut. They gawped at the officers, a man and a woman, who stared back. Ichabod knew them. They'd attended the same school, although he hadn't been friends with them as such. Róisín Clancy and Tommy O'Neal.

Róisín, her blonde hair in a severe, tight bun at the back of her head, had a hard look to her this year, or maybe that was her uniform giving that illusion. Even though Ichabod knew her outside of her uniform as a bubbly woman in the past, he still grew uneasy at the sight of her in it. And Tommy. Any police presence was unwanted this close to the murders. But wasn't it better that Ichabod was here to see and hear things firsthand rather than through gossip later down the line? And he could read faces, spot what the garda weren't saying.

Róisín jerked her head at the Sullivans' table. "Not in here, so?"

So they hadn't found the bodies yet? Or was Róisín playing a game to see who said what? Ichabod watched her closely. Yes, she was playing a game. The bodies had been discovered.

"No," an older lady muttered. "Pretty obvious they're not."

"But they were supposed tae be," Róisín observed, "because the table's empty."

Aoife stomped out from behind the bar and stood in front of Róisín, glaring up at her, hands on hips. "If somethin's happened, just spit it out, cailín. No messin' about."

Ichabod didn't think Róisín would like being called 'girl' in front of everyone, reducing her important status back to who she'd been before she'd taken the pledge, but Aoife wouldn't give a shiny shite about that. She saw people as people, not what they did for a living or who they **thought** they were.

Ichabod put on his poker face, keeping his sights well away from Biffy and his brothers—one wrong move, and the garda might see.

"What's the craic?" Aoife asked. "Comin' in here, spoilin' a damn good night without an explanation. Ye know how it works in this village. Up front and honest with ye words unless ye're in a feud."

Tommy O'Neal stepped forward, clearly a tad unsure as to whether he ought to muscle in or not, considering the landlady was in attack mode. "No need to get lairy, Aoife."

"I'll get as lairy as I feckin' like, and well ye know it, son. I'll be tellin' ye mother if ye think ye can be talkin' tae me like this. I knew ye when ye were in nappies, and don't ye forget it."

"Just doin' our jobs," Tommy mumbled, his cheeks turning pink.

Róisín took over. "Have the Sullivans been in tonight?"

"No," Aoife snapped. "And what of it? Maybe Caoimhe took a tumble and they're after takin' her tae the hospital."

"A tumble?" Róisín asked, all suspicious. "What would ye be knowin' about that?"

Aoife scoffed. "I run the village pub. I know a lot of things. Plus, as ye've lived here all ye life, ye'd know Caoimhe is one of my best friends."

Róisín gave her the side-eye.

"Ye're pissin' me off, so ye are, wid ye hoity-toity garda stare, Miss Fancy Clancy, when ye came from nothin' and shouldn't be flingin' around yer newfound airs and graces—I don't appreciate it." Aoife tapped her foot. "If ye must know, Caoimhe has a muscle wastin' disease, it got worse suddenly, and she falls regularly. I doubt very much Lorcan or his lads would bother tellin' me tae let someone else take their seats, they'd be more inclined tae get her help, as it should be.

So why don't ye go on up to the farm and ask them, or maybe check wid the hospital?"

"We've been to the farm." Róisín reined in her sneer to address everyone else. *"Have ye been in here all evenin'?"*

"Bar Rabbit and the lovely Maeve who arrived not long after seven." Aoife gave Ichabod an apologetic smile.

With all eyes on Ichabod, the meat and tattie pie threatened to come up. He wasn't usually afraid in this kind of situation as he had the twins to back him up in London, but here, he had no one to rely on but himself in this particular situation. He swallowed. Remembered what George and Greg had taught him: how to act, how to appear innocent, how to get himself out of a bind.

Róisín stared his way, assessing, looking down her nose at him. *"Where were ye before here? From five onwards?"*

"Wid me," Granny said unexpectedly.

Despite praying she wouldn't earlier, Ichabod thanked the Lord she'd had a lucid moment.

Granny smiled and patted his arm. *"He's been such a good boy, puttin' my washin' away and cleanin' my kitchen. They broke the mould when he was made."*

Titters went round from the younger people, but the older ones nodded at Ichabod with respect for looking after his gran. There would be a fair few of the youth being told off later—they were expected to stick to the old ways, respecting their elders.

"Who else is due here but hasn't come?" Róisín asked.

Aoife gestured around. "All the tables except that one's filled, so work it out for yeself, cailín."

Róisín gazed at the customers. "Not everyone has a seat, so more could be arrivin' soon. I know full well people just nip in unannounced."

Aoife shook her head in derision. "Are ye sayin' ye're expectin' someone tae come in here? What's happened?"

Róisín ignored her. "Did anyone take the Corduroy Road on the way here, past the back of the Sullivan farm?"

No one answered.

Aoife folded her arms, finally appearing worried. "Is Caoimhe all right, Tommy?"

Ichabod wanted to smirk at Aoife blatantly disregarding Róisín as a source of information. It reminded him of how George behaved, dismissive. Blunt. No fecks to give. The landlady didn't get on with the Clancy family, something about an old feud back in the day that wasn't anything to do with the Gallaghers, but she'd latched on to the Ahearns' side anyway, and she held grudges forever, even if certain people weren't directly involved, like Róisín. Just the fact she was a Clancy would have got her back up.

"No, she's not," Tommy said. "None of them are."

Aoife blanched. "Well? Are ye goin' tae tell us what's up? Maybe we can help? I should be gettin' over there if Caoimhe's poorly."

Tommy glanced at Róisín as if for permission, which Ichabod found weird. Tommy had never been the submissive type, so maybe Róisín was a sergeant now and above him in rank. She dipped her head at him as affirmation that he could take over, then walked out.

Everyone waited for an explanation. The Silvers, probably realising this could go on for some time, stepped off the dais and approached the bar. Aoife didn't go back behind it to serve them, so a reluctant barmaid did it. Tommy, clearly uncomfortable about being put on the spot, shuffled from foot to foot.

"They've all been shot," he said to the flickering flames and cuffed one of his eyes. He'd been good friends with Darragh. "So if ye hear anythin', let us know."

Aoife let out a shriek. "No, not my Caoimhe. Please God, no."

Tommy left, and the whole place erupted. Conversations sprang up, and people chatted about it as though Caldraich had never had a murder before, many shocked exclamations, and someone blurted that 'this kind of thing just doesn't happen in a small village like this'. When it did. Everyone knew that, they just chose to pretend it didn't. Several folks skipped their gazes over the Doyles, and it was obvious by their expressions that they thought the siblings had arranged for it to be done. And that unspoken agreement lingered, that the real reason for the Sullivans' deaths wouldn't be discussed in front of them.

The drugs on Burn Bridge.

Yes, Lorcan must have told a lot of people.

Shite.

Ichabod got Granny settled in bed. She'd had a few gins and fell asleep quickly. Downstairs, he tidied the kitchen to make it look like he'd done it earlier, then entered the living room and added some kindling to the fire. He used the poker to prod the flames back into violent, crackling life. Tossed the balaclava and gloves into the orange flickers and sat on her chair to wait for them to burn.

About five minutes later, a knock came at the front door, and he stiffened, his heartrate escalating. Was it the Doyles? But it could be his auntie, coming back from bingo. Because the light was on, she'd want to check if everything was all right with Granny, whose house would usually be in darkness by now.

He placed the fireguard on the hearth and went to see who was there.

Róisín and Tommy.

Just what I feckin' need.

His heart went like the clappers, and he swallowed his unease.

"Are ye stayin' here the night?" Róisín asked, notebook out and pen poised in the light of the lamp beside the door.

Ichabod nodded. "I thought I'd better. Granny had tae much tae drink. I don't want her gettin' up and fallin' wid no one here tae see tae her."

"Can we come in and have a word?"

Ichabod could say no, he didn't want their voices waking his granny, but what was the point? He may as well get this over with. It wasn't like he hadn't been expecting it. He stepped back, waiting for them to walk inside and disappear into the living room. A deep breath later and he followed them, finding Róisín staring at the fire and Tommy's attention on the carpet.

What was going through their minds? Was Róisín going to play a game again and see if he provided information without being asked? Did she expect him to be like other suspects who created such an elaborate story to cover their tracks that it sounded ridiculous?

Ichabod closed the lounge door and sat in Granny's chair. He slung his legs out in a casual pose. "What's the story?"

Róisín gave him a tight smile that didn't suit her. "I want tae double-check where ye were before goin' tae the Fiddler's." She made eye contact. Gone was the girl he knew, replaced by this…this woman. A stranger.

Then it made sense. She was a Clancy, he was an Ahearn. They weren't supposed to like each other or be civil. Ichabod had lived for so long in the UK that he'd learned despite differences, you could still get along. That didn't apply here, and he'd do well to remember that. Still, he'd be polite to her, put her on the back foot. Show her he could be the bigger person, even if she didn't want to do the same.

"Ye already know that. Like my granny said, I was here. Arrived about ten tae five. She watched a bit of telly while I tidied around."

"How long were ye here before ye went tae the pub?"

She's tryin' tae trip me up. *"Again, ye know that. Two hours or so."*

"And then what?"

He frowned. *"What do ye mean, and then what? We sat in the feckin' pub, had dinner, and then ye two came in. What more is there tae tell?"*

So much for being the bigger person. He'd allowed himself to get arsey with her too easily.

"Why so tetchy?" she asked.

"Because ye've come here tae get answers when ye already know them. It feels like ye're singlin' me out."

Róisín wrote something down. *"Why are ye back in Ireland?"*

Ichabod rolled his eyes. *"I appreciate ye're doin' ye job, but for feck's sake, ye know I come back once or twice a year tae see my family."*

"When was the last time ye came?"

"The same week last year."

"What do ye do in London?"

Now this was where the lies came in. He couldn't mention the twins. What they did, who they were, would land him in hot water, where he'd become a suspect.

"I do odd jobs. A bit of labourin', brickie work, that kind of thing."

She folded her arms. "Have ye heard of the Directorates?"

What the hell is she on about? *"Eh? Who the feck are they?"*

"Do ye know what they do?"

"Err, if I've just made it clear I've never heard of them, how would I know?"

"Ye might have come across them in London. That's where they're from."

He laughed. "It's a big place, Róisín. Millions of people live there. I've got a small flat in one little pocket, and I don't mix well wid others, so I keep tae myself."

"So ye weren't sent over here by them or anythin'? Tae shoot the Sullivans?"

"Why the feck would I shoot farmers?" *He shook his head. "Ye're barkin' up the wrong tree, so ye are. Whoever these Dictators are, they're nothin' tae do wid me."*

"Directorates."

"Whatever. I came tae see my kin, nothin' more."

She relaxed a little, letting her arms drop to her sides, notebook in one hand, pen in the other. "Have ye had anythin' tae do wid the Sullivans since ye got back?"

Here we go. Someone's said I sat at their table. *"I had a drink or three wid them last night. Got caught up in a chat about how they're lookin' tae expand the farm, get some pigs in because the wheat isn't as lucrative anymore."*

"They were lookin'."

Ichabod frowned for effect. "Eh?"

"They're all dead." She stared at him, likely hoping to catch some kind of emotional reaction.

"How was I supposed tae know that? In the pub, Tommy here said they'd been shot. He didn't say they'd died."

Róisín appeared to accept she couldn't pin anything on him. Yet. "Right, so. When are ye goin' back tae London?"

"Sunday, as planned. Why?"

"Just checkin'. How did ye get here? Boat or plane?"

"Plane. Going home the same way. Listen, Lorcan told me last night that someone's doin' drug swaps on Burn Bridge. Said the police were in the know. Maybe these people found out that the Sullivans knew about it and wanted tae keep them quiet."

"That's exactly what I think."

"Right, so go and find them. It's nothin' tae do wid me." Ichabod stood.

Róisín glanced at Tommy who finally lifted his gaze from the carpet. She returned her focus to Ichabod. "We'll be watchin' ye."

Tommy tutted.

Ichabod laughed. "There's nothin' tae see here. Nothin' at all."

Chapter Nine

Katy Marlborough was her usual irritating self, overexuberant and just plain annoying, the tinkling laugh Ichabod hated *so much* grating on his last nerve. It was fake, he was sure of it. Something she'd created in a bid to make herself appear coquettish. She'd dressed to the nines in a skin-tight, slinky black dress with a long slit up one side that reached her groin, showing off that she didn't have underwear on, unless it was a thong. He supposed her flash of leg was meant to tickle his pickle. It didn't. Nor did her excessive use of makeup. He preferred Marleigh and the less-is-more look.

Katy's high heels clicked on the pavement, tapping an incessant beat in his head, her handbag further pissing him off by slapping the front of his thigh with each step. He walked beside her down the busy night-time street Up West, her arm linked with his—far too familiar for his liking, but he'd have to grin and bear it. This was a job, and it required him to get information. That may not be achievable if he acted mardy.

All the way here in the taxi, she'd prattled on about her life with no mention of any grief she experienced regarding her sister, Josephine, and nephew, Chesney. She either acted chirpy to hide it or she didn't care they were gone. Odd, whatever the reason. As an Irishman who'd gone to a few funerals back home, he was used to grief being out in the open. Then again, hadn't he learned to not let it outwardly affect him since he'd climbed the Cardigan ladder? Hadn't Aoife been a shuttered window?

Marleigh's words came back to him. *"People lie to cover the hurts inside."*

Up West wasn't somewhere he'd have chosen to take Katy, but she'd insisted on it. Clearly a money-grabber, or at least a woman who liked to be wined and dined as if she were a queen. Ichabod thanked his lucky stars the twins had given him a chunk of money as expenses. God knew how much this meal was going to cost.

She trotted into Vincenchie's, an exclusive Italian restaurant, and the gentlemanly part of him bristled that she hadn't waited to let him hold the door for her. But she wasn't on his romantic radar, so did it really matter? And maybe she was an independent woman who didn't appreciate the old-fashioned ways.

There was more of Caldraich in him than he'd realised. Liverpool and London hadn't erased the core teachings of that village.

Katy waltzed up to the podium where a man in a black tux stood, smiling. His gold nametag bore the words *Signor Jacquard*.

"Can I help you, modom?" he asked in plum English.

Modom? Feckin' hell. It's one of those *places*.

"A reservation for two under Katy Marlborough." She treated him to one of her bugging laughs.

Jacquard (which sounded decidedly French) smiled tightly. It appeared the laugh annoyed him as much as it did Ichabod. "Signor Smith will escort you."

Another man in a tux stepped out of nowhere and treated Katy to a knowing smile. His thin body gave him a gangly appearance, his black curls resembling the floret tops of broccoli. His face would be handy for someone who gurned for a living, the skin a little like plasticine. All in all, he was odd.

"Smith!" Katy said. "How lovely to *see* you."

"Ms Marlborough." He may as well have bowed. "If you'd like to come this way…"

He led them through a plethora of diners who'd put on their glad rags, not to mention a lot of slap, red lipstick predominant. Many a Rolex or Tag Heuer hugged wrists, cufflinks with diamonds sparkling in the light of wavering candle flames, women's hair glossy down their backs. People here had money—a lot of it.

Muted conversation plucked at Ichabod's eardrums—he'd gone into work mode, picking up words in case they were useful to the twins.

"Oh, the Bentley, darling. I simply won't arrive in anything else…"

"Did you *see* the way he treated me? I rather think he ought to get the sack…"

"We must visit dear Verity at school this weekend. I still feel dreadful that we spent Christmas away from her when she's only six…"

Ichabod almost paused at that to tell them, if they were talking about their child, what a pair of utter bollock-bastards they were to leave her at boarding school at this time of year, especially when she was so young. But it wasn't his problem, so he moved on, offering up a prayer that Verity didn't come out of this a damaged adult.

Smith ended their journey in the far-left corner beneath a low, sloping ceiling, a table set apart from the others in an obvious way. Secluded. Private. Had Katy been here before to know of its existence? She must have—she knew Smith. Had she specifically requested it when she'd phoned to book? Was that her thing, preying on men and getting them to treat her here? Was Vincenchie's a regular haunt? Intel had come in about her that she slept around, but this was on another level. She was an outright prospector, digging for gold.

It narked him he might be one of many men she used—or more specifically, she thought he was stupid enough to fall for her. He recalled a conversation they'd had in The Angel, where he'd told her he didn't fancy her—he was desperate to make her feck off, leave him alone. But she wouldn't have it. She had a high opinion of herself and thought every man wanted her—or they should. Perhaps that was why she didn't have a long-term relationship on the go. Men spotted her conceitedness and ran a mile.

Like he'd tried to.

They sat, Smith wafting his bony hand in a flourish, taking napkins off the table and making a big show of snapping them from their intricate, origami folds to lay them on their laps.

Uncomfortable in such a posh place, his anger at being in this situation when Marleigh was home, alone, worrying about tomorrow, sent Ichabod's blood pressure soaring. He wanted to tell Smith to feck off to Fecksville then feck off again, but he held himself in check.

Finally, the man handed them menus, one for food, one for wine. "I'll give you a few minutes." He sauntered off, pausing at a nearby table to ask the customers if everything was all right, just as a woman had put food into her mouth.

One of Ichabod's many bugbears, that. How the feck could you reply with a wedge of steak between your teeth?

Katy went for the wine menu first. Of course she did. He sensed she was pretending what to choose because she opted for a whole bottle of Bollinger pretty quickly. It zipped him right back to another time he'd tasted the stuff, in a weird little office with a man called Solly Moss, a leader in North London. He swept the memory away and browsed the dishes on offer. Eyes wide at the prices, he had to compose himself. No wonder the twins had given him a few hundred quid for this meal.

Katy beamed across from him. "The food here is to die for."

Then enjoy it, because it could be ye last bit of grub.

Ichabod supposed he ought to smile. "I wouldn't know. I'm more of a Burger King man."

She tittered. "Oh, you're so *silly*!"

"I love a Whopper."

"Don't we all, darling."

She eyed him in what she must have thought a tempting manner. It did nothing but leave him stone-cold. He dipped his head to break away from her intense, pervy gaze, trying to work out what was what on the menu. Why couldn't they just put 'starter' and 'dinner'? Why did it have to be in Italian? Each meal also had an Italian name, and he had to read the description below to know what it was.

He didn't belong here.

He opted for mozzarella sticks to start and the plainest dinner he could find, one that appeared on most people's tables at home. Bolognaise, except here it was called Semplice Ragu, and the pasta had a fancy name, reginette. Whatever it was, he'd bet it wasn't spaghetti. He'd hoped to eat that so he could make a mess of himself, put Katy off him sexually by getting it all over his fake beard which, feck, he'd forgotten to take off prior to coming here. Hadn't she even noticed it? Was she *that* self-absorbed? Or maybe, because she knew he worked for the twins, it was a given that he'd be in disguise sometimes. He caught sight of the words *tagliatelle carbonara* and smiled. While he wouldn't have red sauce splashes on his suit, he would have cream ones. A dollop of that on his black tie would stand out a mile.

He turned the page, only to be confronted with set specials. "Where's the afters?"

Katy raised her eyebrows. "That's a *separate* menu here, darling, and it's desserts, not afters."

If she calls me darlin' one more time...

"Grand." He didn't despise himself for not knowing how these fancy places worked. He was proud of his roots and what he'd been taught, much preferring a menu to just state what the feck was on offer so he could pick out his whole meal in one go. Now he'd have to wait until dinner was over before he could see what the *desserts* were. Unless... "What sort of puddin' do they have?"

"Lemon tart, profiteroles, tiramisu, cannoncini..."

"What the feck's that?"

"Pastry horny—sorry, *horns*—filled with cream and ricotta whipped together."

He ground his teeth at her intentional slip. If he could rip the twins a new arsehole for sending him here with her, he would. "I'll have the lemon tart."

"A man after my own heart."

Err, no, ye geebag. An appropriate word, as it described an annoying woman. He laughed, forcing himself to play her game. If she thought he liked her, she'd be more forthcoming in the info department.

Smith glided back. "Are you ready to order, sir, modom?"

Katy took over, and Ichabod was glad to let her. Smith floated away again, inciting another memory in Solly Moss' office of that creepy feck, Bonce, a butler type who'd put him on edge. Ichabod packed it away into a compartment he tried to keep locked, but speaking to Marleigh about some of his past had meant the lid was ajar, things creeping out. Solly was linked to the Ireland murders, so it was inevitable Ichabod would remember him so vividly.

The Bolly arrived. Smith poured, giving wonky smiles and wide-eyed glances coupled with strange nods, reminding Ichabod of Rowan Atkinson. Once the man had gone away, Ichabod took a sip, transported back to being in Solly's company.

"A bit of a celebration…"

Go away, ye weird bastard.

Katy launched into conversation. Ichabod found he didn't have to reply all that often, giving her a bob of the head here and there, the occasional *hmm* and *ah*. She was quite content to talk about herself, and his mind wandered. She'd been spoken to after Josephine and Chesney had died, hadn't seemed to know anything about their drug office or what they did. She'd said they dealt in antiques as Josephine's house was apparently full of old things, but maybe that was what she'd been told to say.

The starters came and went, Ichabod's mozzarella sticks more like giant fish fingers in size, and he worked out the were six-fifty a pop, and he had three. How did this place get away with that kind of markup? In the smidgen of time between that and dinner, she waffled on and on, only pausing when more food arrived. Smith placed a risotto containing mussels in front of Katy and the carbonara down for Ichabod. They ate, Katy talking about furniture in between bites.

"And I sold it for sixteen thousand," she said.

"What, a curio cabinet sold for that much?"

She nodded. "I know Josephine's estate hasn't officially passed to me yet, but it's coming to me anyway so I may as well dispose of all the things

I don't like. I'm the only surviving relative. I knew she was into antiques but didn't realise her tat was worth so much. I'm moving into her house next week so want to get rid of the things that aren't to my taste."

"So ye think she got all her money from buyin' and sellin' old stuff?"

Katy paused, her vivaciousness fading for a second before it sprang back up and she offered him a sly smile. "Well…"

"Well what?"

"Here's where I need your help."

Ichabod's heartbeat ratcheted up. "Right…"

"Do you happen to know anyone who'd run a side business I've recently become aware of?"

Does she literally want a name or is she askin' me tae do it?

And it all made sense now. He'd wondered why she supposedly fancied him, when he didn't think he was much to look at. It was obvious she'd only been pretending because of what he could do for her. She must have thought flattery would secure whatever deal she wanted to make with him. At least Marleigh had been up front about that, how she worried she was using him.

Katy was more of a snake, though, so wouldn't have disclosed that sort of information.

"Something to do with Josephine," she breezed on. "I'd like the revenue stream from it but haven't got the faintest idea how to go about working in that sort of line. I *snorted* when I found out what had been going on. A little *weed* of a teenager came to the office while I was there clearing it out. He seemed to think I was some kind of *heroine,* that I'd save him because he thought his usual source had dried up once Josephine and Chesney died."

More intentional slips. Something she could deny if he pulled her up on it, but she was referring to drugs, he was sure of it.

"I think I know what ye're sayin'. Have ye approached The Brothers about this? Ye do know they'd need tae take protection money, don't ye?" He let a ribbon of tagliatelle fall and slap onto his tie.

"Oh, what a messy boy you are!" That titter. She reached across, picked off the pasta, and popped it in her mouth, sucking on her finger.

Am I supposed tae find that sexy? A gross wagon, so she is. Another term for an annoying woman. He was full of them tonight. "Sorry. Like I said,

Burger King man." He ate the last bits of ham or whatever the hell was in his meal. "So have ye? Spoken tae the twins?"

"No." A dark look passed over her features then disappeared quickly. She brightened. "I don't want to share the profits."

Got ye, ye cute hoor. "So what do ye need me for?"

"I've had a rather unsettling conversation on the phone with a man calling himself Daggers." She shook her head in disdain. "I'm sure that name was supposed to frighten me, as was him having my number. I hadn't switched my mobile on for a while, and there were several threatening messages. From what he said, he can't have got the memo that Josephine is dead. Anyway, he said she owes him for the latest *gear* and he'll be coming tomorrow to collect, he'd waited long enough. I'd like you to tell him I don't have the money at the moment and negotiate some kind of deal to make him go away, give me some breathing space. After all, *I* didn't order the stuff from him, Josephine did, so it really isn't my problem. Of course, now I've decided to step in where she left off, that would include getting more *product*, so you'd have to persuade him to trust us, and unfortunately, I'll have to pay off her debt."

"But I work for the twins, ye know that."

"Yes, but everyone likes a side hustle, don't they? A little secret to keep? I want you to help me run the business. You're into martial arts, so you'll be able to protect me."

"Okay, I'm in, but if The Brothers find out, I'm goin' tae throw ye tae the dogs. Make out I didn't have anythin' tae do wid it."

She pouted. "*That* isn't very nice."

"I have tae protect myself. They're hard bastards, and I'm fond of my kneecaps."

Smith suddenly appeared to take away their pasta bowls. Katy stared at Ichabod, perhaps sizing him up. Then Smith came back with the dessert menus.

Without looking at him, she said, "We don't need those, darling. Two lemon tarts." She knocked back her champagne as Smith drifted away. She nodded. "We're not going to get caught, so I accept your terms. You won't need to drop me in the doo-dah. So!" She poured more fizz. "Let's cheers to a new adventure."

He raised his glass to hers.

Cheers tae ye death, soith. (Bitch.)

Chapter Ten

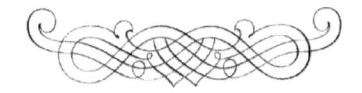

Katy, pleased she'd secured Ichabod as her fall guy, someone to take the blame if the drug office ever got raided by the police, glanced through the passenger-side window at the dark, empty road in the East End. She'd have his name put on the agreement as renting the office, without his knowledge, of course. She knew a man who knew a man, and it would be done under the table with money secretly changing hands.

"Where are we going? This isn't the way to my house." She wasn't frightened, more intrigued.

Ichabod was one of those dense Irishmen who wouldn't have it in him to do anything cruel to her, no matter that he was prepared to get rough for The Brothers. He couldn't even handle her salacious talk, blushing, fumbling over his words, so raising a hand to a woman wasn't in his repertoire. Besides, she was gorgeous, so why *would* he turn on her?

"Just got tae stop off for a sec tae show ye somethin'."

He parked at the kerb outside a line of warehouses, their high windows blacked out. Going by the geography of the area in her head, they backed onto the Thames. A memory prodded at the recesses of her mind, but she couldn't grab hold of it. She was sozzled, so maybe that was why.

He unclipped his seat belt. "Come in wid me. There are a few things inside that will help wid the business."

She leaned closer, hoping for a kiss. "*Our* business."

"Yeah, that."

He left her pouting lips and got out, rounding the car. Annoyed he hadn't done what she wanted, she told herself she'd have to ramp it up with this man. Go the extra mile. She didn't mind the chase if the reward was worth it, and judging by what she'd found out online, drugs were a lucrative business. She had to keep him onside if she wanted to fill her coffers.

Before she had a chance to join Ichabod on the pavement, he'd opened her door. Well, this was nice. She hadn't encountered a gentleman in a while, not since that old man who'd told her he was eighty but he'd looked more like a hundred. Mind you, his good manners had soon disappeared. She'd been prepared to suck his wrinkly sausage for his money, but he'd turned his nose up at her stroking his leg at the dinner table, getting up and leaving her to foot the bill.

Some men were so disrespectful, weren't they?

She stepped out, ensuring the slit of her dress parted sufficiently to expose the long length of her slim leg. By the time they got to her place later, Ichabod wouldn't be able to resist her. She'd bind him to her with sex. Let loose her kinky side so he couldn't get enough of her. He'd think with his cock not his head, and she could manipulate him into doing whatever she wanted.

He took her arm and guided her to some iron-pole gates. Beyond them, a car park with a battered white van bearing a logo on the side: *Easy Logistics*. Was someone else here?

"Whose is that?" she asked.

"Mine. I use it tae ferry things about."

"What things?"

"I'll tell ye in a minute." He took keys out of his pocket and undid a padlock, leading her into the car park then securing the gates again.

Why did he need to do that if it was only them here?

Maybe he's worried someone will burst in and steal something.

She glanced at the warehouse. "What's in there?"

"Let's just say ye picked the right person tae do business wid. I'm already in the trade, I just didn't want tae say it in the restaurant wid that Smith fella loiterin' about. Many listenin' ears were in there, ye know. This is where I keep my stash."

Already in the trade? Well, who knew? Josephine must be looking out for her up there. "A pretty big place. Do you have quite a bit of product, then?" She paused. Vaguely recalled rumours about a warehouse but, after drinking almost a whole bottle of Bolly, she couldn't tie the memory to anyone.

Should she be worried?

Of course not. This is Ichabod we're talking about here.

"Just had a shipment," he said. "Instead of dealin' wid that Daggers fella, *I'll* sell ye the stuff."

"Oh goody." *This is going better than I thought.*

She clapped, eager to set eyes on the packages, to later roll in the money the drugs would bring. All those clothes she could buy. Shoes. Jewellery. And she'd get a fancy new car straight off the line. She'd always envied Josephine her considerable wealth, and now she knew where it had come from. Things hadn't worked out as well for Katy. The men she'd targeted had cottoned on quickly that she was only after what they could give her—she really ought to rethink her strategy. It wasn't as easy to snag someone now she was older. She had money, just not as much as she wanted. Now was her chance to become rich.

He pressed a code into a keypad, and the door clicked open. She eyed a small square hallway and another door to the right.

Ichabod went inside and turned the handle on the second door. "Are ye comin' in, or would ye prefer tae freeze ye tits off?"

"There are many things I'd like done to my tits, but freezing isn't one of them."

He didn't laugh, but she did to cover her embarrassment.

She trotted inside, almost twisting an ankle in her haste. Ichabod went through the second doorway, and she closed the first one then followed him. She stared to the right at a long table, tools on top. What were they for? Three stacks of fold-out chairs rested against the back wall beside a strange metal contraption that appeared to be created from spikes. Should she be here? Was this on the level? She swept those thoughts away and did an inventory of the things she hadn't looked at yet. To the left, a sofa, a TV in front of it. She recognised a set of Xbox headphones the same as a pair she'd bought for Chesney one Christmas. Did Ichabod play *games* while here? Was he a little boy at heart?

Oh dear. Hardly the type I'd want to take to bed.

Still, she could find someone else later on for a more permanent relationship. And if she didn't, she'd enjoy screwing them in bed along the way. Men never turned her down when sex was on the table—apart from that old man, *and* Ichabod that night in The Angel, but she wouldn't dwell on that. She hadn't believed him when he'd said he wasn't interested in her anyway. And she'd been right, because he'd just spent close to four hundred pounds on dinner and drinks, so he must want to get into her knickers. Men didn't part with that kind of cash if they didn't want to peek at your muffin.

She glanced around for pallets with packages on top, as she'd imagined that was how drugs were stored, a square pile of them covered in clingfilm. But there wasn't a pallet in sight, nor were there boxes or suitcases. There *were* two doors on the right-hand wall, though. Perhaps the bounty was in there.

"Show me the money," she quipped.

Ichabod smiled. "We need tae discuss the terms first." His voice echoed in the large space. "Let me just go over what I propose. The initial offer from ye was for me tae work for ye in the drug office Josephine ran wid Chesney. I would talk tae the Daggers fella and ask him tae wait until ye had the funds tae pay him for what Josephine must have had on tick. And ye wanted me tae ask him for more product, again on tick. Have I got that right?"

"Yes." Why was he going over it again?

"I agreed tae do that but then brought ye here. Instead, I'm offerin' tae pay off Daggers and provide the gear. Ye can pay me back out of the profits. Does that suit ye?"

"God, yes!"

"Give me Daggers' phone number, then."

She took her phone out of her bag and found the beastly man in her contact list. She showed Ichabod the screen, and he popped the number into his mobile.

"If ye go against this agreement, I'll grass ye up tae the twins," he said.

"That's fair, I suppose."

"Right, let me show ye the goods." He walked to one of the doors and pushed it open. "It's in there. Go and have a gander, see what ye think."

She glanced at him to check for any signs of duplicity and found none.

One step, two steps, three, then she was in a bathroom.

The door slammed shut, revealing who'd stood behind it.

"We heard every damning word, Katy," George said, his twin by his side.

Oh fuck.

Chapter Eleven

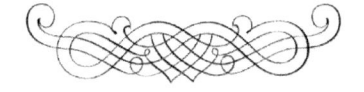

George didn't want to expend *too* much energy on Katy Marlborough, not when he had the David debacle going on tomorrow, but it wouldn't stop him from being a cruel bastard to her. He had a reason for doing it, one Greg was aware of.

The woman had said she wasn't prepared to pay protection money, and that was enough for them to kill her. All right, she hadn't actually dealt any drugs since Josephine's death—that she'd admitted to anyway—but the fact she'd planned to was another reason to cut her life short.

To be fair, he'd kill her just for being related to that bitch. Hardly right, but Katy had been a pest regarding Ichabod for a while, too, keep bugging him for dates, and she'd muffed things up in The Angel on the night they'd arranged to nab the Slasher, a serial killer intent on murdering Lillibet, one of Debbie's girls, amongst others. Katy preventing Ichabod from leaving the pub and going after the Slasher had meant the bloke had got away.

George couldn't forgive her for that.

As usual with captives, they'd tied her to the wooden chair using rope, her arms trapped by her sides. Prior to that, George had forced her to remove her clothes, a nice little indignity she'd suffered through, cheeks blazing, her back to them as though that would preserve her modesty. Funny how she'd wanted to get Ichabod into bed, show him her nakedness, yet hadn't liked it when the time had come—served her right for all those inuendoes she'd thrown at him about sex. Of course, stripping for bedroom antics was entirely different to stripping for death, but whatever.

Ichabod played on the Xbox with Greg, so George had the floor to himself. This was a done-and-dusted issue already, he didn't need to torture her for a confession, but he fancied playing with her for a bit before he administered the fatal slice.

"Enjoy your dinner, did you?" he asked her.

She nodded, panic contorting her expression. Urine swelled in the gap between her legs, dark yellow, gravitating towards her knees then dripping over, a piss waterfall.

He smiled. "Do we get a thank you?"

"W-what do you mean?"

"Me and my brother paid for that nosh, so the least you can do is be grateful for it. Only polite, isn't it?"

"I…I am. It was l-lovely."

"Take many men there to feed your greedy gold-digger guts, do you?"

"I-I go on d-dates there, yes."

"Dates. Is that what that was tonight? Ah, and there was me thinking you were going to use Ichabod to run your business for you."

"I...I didn't mean any of it."

"So why say it?"

"I don't know."

"You're lying."

She had the grace to blush.

He had the urge to punch her nose and break it. Listen to the crunch. "You sound scared. I suppose *I* would be if I sat where you are and some big bastard stood in front of me. What d'you reckon is going to happen now?"

"You'll beat me up for going behind your back."

She'd sounded so confident about that. She really didn't know what she'd walked into. The mistake she'd made.

He paced back and forth. "Is that what you think? Interesting. So that's all you believe you deserve? Is your opinion of yourself that high? Don't bother answering. It's yes. You love yourself, don't you. More than the average person."

"Please don't hurt me."

"I'm not going to bother lying to you. What I do *will* hurt. Blades tend to. You must know how it feels when you cut yourself while chopping veg. It stings. Bleeds."

"Why am I here?"

"Come on now. You know why. See, not only have you been a naughty girl, but there are the sins of Dickie Feathers, Josephine, and Chesney to talk about. I mean, none of them paid us protection money either. Dickie I can understand, he was a knob who thought he could do whatever he wanted, but your sister and nephew—and you? Does your family always flout the rules?"

"I didn't know about the drugs at first. I swear, I thought they dealt in antiques."

"Yet when you received that phone call from Daggers, you jumped at the opportunity to sell drugs without consulting us first. We'll find out who he is by his phone number; our copper will run a trace on who pays the bill, and he'll be brought here to answer for himself, like you."

She gave him a belligerent stare. "I don't see why you should have protection money. It's not like you'd send one of your men to the office all day and night, is it? To actually *protect* me."

"No, because the payment is for *your* protection against *us*. Being upfront about what you're doing and paying us a cut means we won't kill you. Sadly, you skipped that part, so here we are."

"I'll pay it. I'll do whatever you want."

"The time for that has long gone, sunshine. You were a prick, thinking you could outsmart us. Those who make that mistake end up in the Thames. Chopped up into little bits. You'll see for yourself soon. I'll cut a slice so you can see exactly how you'll end up. You'll pass out shortly after that—the pain, you know how it goes—but it'll give you an idea what'll go on when you're unconscious."

"You'd do it while I'm *alive*?"

He smiled. "I'm nice like that. Wouldn't even charge you to view it. People would pay good money to watch, you know, and here's you, getting it for free. You ought to be grateful."

George wandered into the bathroom and collected a forensic outfit. He put it on to protect his grey suit—for the most part now, he covered his own clothing to save getting an earful from Greg who'd become sick of burning their stuff in the fire at home and forking out for new gear.

He left the room and went over to the tool table, taking his time, liking the idea of Katy crapping herself and not being able to turn her head far enough to see what he was doing. The sounds of gunfire coming from the telly and

Ichabod calling Greg an eejit for presumably shooting his character brought on a wince. Greg being shot for real in that abattoir, George would never get over it.

The Irishman had been invaluable lately, leaving his role at Jackpot Palace at the drop of a hat to run to their aid. Whatever they asked of him, he did it. He already got paid a good wedge, but George reckoned he deserved another one, elevating him past the next level and into top-tier wages.

Some people were just that good.

Ichabod would need the extra pay if he managed to snag Marleigh as his bird. That woman was used to the high life. Could he handle her?

Not my problem—unless she becomes one.

George concentrated on the job at hand. He selected one of his latest buys, a large yellow woodwork clamp. Standing in front of Katy, he turned it so the frame resembled a C. He rested the up-curve of the C's base beneath her right jawline.

"This bit of the clamp is called a fixed jaw," he informed her, "which is ironic, seeing as I'm about to fix *your* jaw in place."

He settled the upper curve of the C on top of her head. She didn't move, which made things easier, and he wondered why she wasn't struggling. Had she accepted her fate already? He screwed down the handle, and she bloody well moved then as the clamp tightened, closing her mouth. The click of her jawbone stopped him from going further.

"Now then, let's do a bit of art."

He walked back to the table. Picked up a retractable blade knife from a set of two. The reviews had mentioned a man using one to open silage bales, but George would have used them to trim wallpaper. Each to their own. He moved the blade out, pleased it resembled a Stanley knife, and went back to Katy. He held the back of her hair to keep her head steady, then wrote one word on her forehead: TRAITOR. Blood dripped over her eyes, and she closed them, whimpering, not a scream to be heard. She was made of stronger stuff than he'd thought.

Then he carved her cheeks, a deep slice here and there, enough to get the claret flowing. She screamed then. Back at the table, he tossed the blade into a bucket of bleach water and picked up a paintbrush, the kind used for skirting boards and the like.

Katy glared at him when he stood in front of her again, her face a mask of scarlet fluid. He dipped the paintbrush into the T of Traitor and inspected the bristles. Not enough. He soaked more up from her gushing cheeks then swept the blood-paint over the tops of her thighs so she could see the results of his efforts—and to scare her shitless for kicks. She grunted what he imagined had started as a scream, but her closed mouth prevented the sound from reaching its true potential, seeping past her clenched teeth and wobbling lips. He dipped and painted, dipped and painted until the fronts of both legs were covered, ending at her toes. She snorted snot out, her tears meshing with the blood on her face.

"Have you got a headache from that clamp? I'd offer you some Panadol but I'm not in the mood to be generous."

He took the brush to the bucket and collected his circular saw, bored now of toying with her. He placed it on the floor, directly in her view, and her eyes widened, pathetic whines coming out of her.

"Oh, shut your fucking tedious nonsense."

He unscrewed the clamp, and as soon as she could get her mouth open, she screeched. George turned to see the reaction from Greg and Ichabod. Greg carried on playing his game, but the Irishman got up and came over, head cocked, studying her. What was he thinking? George had done this to see how Ichabod took it, his actions designed to incite questions. For George to gauge exactly where the man's head was at now.

"Why bother paintin' her, what was the point?"

"Because I can," George said.

"Why carve that word in her head if no one's goin' tae see it?"

"For fun."

George watched the man for signs of revulsion or the unspoken thought that George was a nutter who enjoyed doing things just because.

"Does it go against your morals?" George asked. "For me to do whatever I want to people because it makes me happy? Calms the savage beast or whatever the fuck you want to call it?"

Ichabod shrugged. "It's none of my business what ye do."

"But I want to know."

Ichabod looked him in the eye. "I don't like how it makes me feel."

"Which is?"

"Happy that her face is wrecked. She was goin' tae go against ye, and that's not allowed."

George nodded. Just what he'd wanted to hear. "Cheers for the input."

Ichabod frowned and stepped back.

George picked up the circular saw and positioned the jagged-tooth blade just above Katy's knee. He leant forward to get maximum blood splash on his face, needing it to remind him of what it had felt like when he'd killed his fake father, Richard. To remind him the man was gone.

He set the tool in motion. The blade bit into her skin, blood and flesh flying, Katy's screams loud, growing hoarse the more he sliced. He reached bone and powered through it to the other side. The lower half of her leg flopped forward and thudded onto the floor, the exposed stump of her thigh gushing blood, shit loads of it pumping out to splash on his shoe covers. He eyed the marrow of her bone, stained from the blood that coasted down over it. She silenced, her chin dropping to her chest, out for the count.

"Thank God she shut up," George muttered. He glanced back at Ichabod. "How did *that* make you feel?"

"Not tae bad. Why do ye need tae know?"

"Because you want to kill David and I need to know if you're in the right headspace. Given the Sullivans and all that went on there—and afterwards, how you beat yourself up—I need you in top-notch condition mentally."

Ichabod's face clouded over with anger. "Oh, I'm ready for him, don't ye worry. I'm ready for whatever ye want tae throw at me."

Good man.

Chapter Twelve

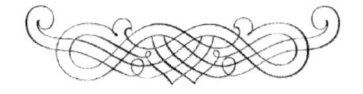

Ichabod left the warehouse and drove to Marleigh's. Despite the late hour, she'd replied to his text, asking if he could come round. Had she been awake all this time, waiting for him? He'd like to think so. Or maybe the loneliness was getting to her again and she just needed him for company. He sighed. Why was he sabotaging every first thought he had? He smiled wryly.

Hadn't he told her the first thought was your true self and the brain tried to override it? What was his brain trying to protect him *from*, though? It didn't help that George had spoken Ichabod's thoughts, as if he'd harvested them from his mind: Marleigh using them to get back at David through spite.

He couldn't wait to see her, to erase Katy from inside his head. He planned to be open and honest about the 'date' and what had come after. The warehouse antics would give Marleigh a taste of exactly who he was becoming.

Someone who didn't mind bloodshed. Screams. Witnessing agony.

How odd, to discover he'd viewed it all so dispassionately, seeing it as part of the job, something he had to excel at in order to climb yet another Cardigan rung. All right, he'd been given Jackpot Palace to run, a huge responsibility, and they always chose him for the important surveillance jobs. But he was desperate to show the twins he was so much more than a casino manager and part-time follow-those-people operative.

What was he saying? That he wanted to be like *them*? Killing?

To stop himself from going down that dark path, he laughed about that time they'd chosen him to fit up that therapist, Janet. If they hadn't, he'd still be a mere foot soldier. Still have a chest of drawers full of skinny jeans and tracksuits. Trainers. What more did *really* he want, though? He wasn't sure. Perhaps for George and Greg to openly say how they valued him? But why did he need that? Why was it so important to get validation when he'd never been the needy type before?

Fecked if I know.

Maybe I'm after erasin' the Sullivans from my mind. If I kill so many more after them, I'll forget what I did tae that family.

He swerved onto Marleigh's driveway, and the garage door rose. She must have set the scanner to accept his number plate. Inordinately pleased about that, her trust in him, he drove inside and cut the engine, then got out. The door lowered, enclosing him in darkness. He blindly moved to another door, the one that opened up into her kitchen, and tapped on it. With no response, he tried the handle, his guts going over in case David was back early and she hadn't told him.

Why would she do that, though?

Don't be an eejit. His car wasn't out the front.

He shrugged off his suspicion and entered the kitchen. She was halfway across the room, clearly on her way to greet him. Her smile melted his heart. It looked genuine. Or was that what he wanted to see?

First thought. It's genuine.

He twisted the key in the lock. "What a feckin' night…"

She glanced at the clock on the wall. "Or early hours of the morning. Let me make you some tea. Or do you need something stronger?"

"Somethin' stronger, but only a small one. I need tae drive tae the airport, remember."

"There's a few hours yet." She turned and opened a cupboard, taking out Bombay gin and a bottle of tonic.

He sat at the island, weary of body but alert of mind. Katy's murder had fired something up in him.

"Tell me," Marleigh said. "Get it off your chest."

So he spoke about Katy, how George had killed her, and then he returned to Ireland.

Chapter Thirteen

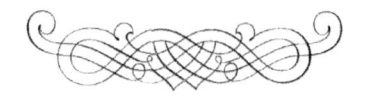

In the red wingback chair, Ichabod woke to the sound of footsteps on the lino in the hallway. They didn't sound like Granny's — no shuffling — but heavy, sure, precise. The lamp was still on, the flames in the grate thinking about going out, grasping on to the last vestiges of life, so some light spilled out through the doorway. He stood, moved stealthily towards the door, bracing himself to attack using his martial arts skills.

At least this time he'd have the advantage and wouldn't have a black sack rammed over his head and be snatched from behind by two or more men.

Tommy O'Neal appeared in the hallway in civvy clothes, staring in at Ichabod with a look of shame mixed with guilt—why, because he'd come in instead of knocking on the front door? He remained on the threshold, glancing to his left, as though someone else was with him and that was the only way he could let Ichabod know. Or maybe someone was in the back garden, waiting. Róisín? Had they done their investigating and someone had seen Ichabod at the farm—or had the Doyles put his name forward to get the heat off themselves? Perhaps he was by himself and worried he'd be seen by someone in a house out the back. But why all the subterfuge?

And how the feck did he get in?

Ichabod sighed. "I wasn't aware the garda came inside people's houses without a warrant or bein' invited."

"It was the only way I could speak to ye in private."

"Got anyone wid ye?"

"No."

"I think I'd like tae see for myself first if it's all the same tae ye."

Ichabod brushed past him, walking down the hallway and into the kitchen. He nosed through the glass in the back door, reaching across to flick the outside light on. No one stood in the garden. He ensured the door was locked, then searched the rest of the house. Granny slept like the dead, snoring. He returned downstairs and peered into the kitchen again in case Tommy had let someone in while he wasn't there, Ichabod's mind working as if he were on a job for The Brothers.

In the living room, he found Tommy sitting in Granny's chair, elbows on his knees, his face in his hands.

"What the feck is goin' on?" Ichabod asked. "Why are ye here?"

Tommy looked up. "Róisín's in wid the Doyles, I'd put money on it. I caught her havin' a conversation with Biffy once when we were at their place regarding Alastar drivin' wid no insurance. I'd gone out the front tae check the vehicle, and when I came back in, I heard more than I'm comfortable wid. She saw me standin' there, told me tae get in the patrol car, and when she got in, she made out she was pretendin' tae be on their side, like she's undercover or somethin'."

Ichabod nodded. "So what happened after that?"

"She told me not tae tell anyone what Biffy had said tae her, about ensurin' the bridge was clear on Thursdays, that all traffic was monitored by her so they had a clear run. I wondered why we kept goin' out there, parkin' on the verge tae apparently catch speeders. That's for the traffic police from Omagh tae do, not us, but she said we'd been assigned that road regardless. Once I heard her wid Biffy, I convinced myself that was part of her undercover thing, but tonight…she didn't speak tae the Doyles before or after we came here tae question ye, yet I told her they should be asked their whereabouts. That's not right, everyone knows they've murdered other people, the garda just can't prove it, so talkin' tae them should be high on our list."

"Why are ye tellin' me this? What's it got tae do wid me?"

"Because I think she's after ye, she's not undercover she's in wid them, and she wants tae blame the Sullivan shooting on ye so the Doyles aren't suspected. All that chatter about the Directorates—if she's on the level and makin' out tae the Doyles that she's a bent copper tae get information out of them, then she'd know about the London drug gang via work, but what if she knows because she's a part of the Doyle outfit? I'm so confused."

Ichabod thought about the instruction he'd been given to leave the gun behind the tractor wheel. Why had Biffy insisted on that? Ichabod hadn't touched it without gloves on, and the gloves were no more, burned in the fire, but he'd still have gunshot residue on his jacket. Feck, he'd need to burn that when Tommy had gone, in case Róisín got it into her head to ask him for it.

"Are ye sayin' she's stringin' ye along about bein' undercover when really she's in wid the Doyles full stop?" he asked.

"I think so, and I don't know what tae do about it."

"Tell your boss?"

Tommy laughed. "Are ye jokin' me? He's her cousin and as dodgy as they come. I heard he takes backhanders and looks the other way."

"Ye're in a bit of a mess, so."

"Hmm. I needed tae warn ye that if she can make it stick, ye'll be brought in."

Ichabod had almost said, "The Doyles don't want me caught for this," but he stopped himself. This could be the real reason Tommy was here, for Ichabod to say that exact thing, a trick to trip him up. "I don't have anythin' tae do wid the Doyles. Remember how they bullied me? They don't like me, so why, hypothetically, would they use me tae gun down the Sullivans? Why *would they trust me? And why would I even do that? It makes no sense."*

"I know, but Róisín's devious. Corrupt, I'm sure of it."

"I don't know what tae say. I'm only here tae see my family. I knew nothin' about the Burn Bridge thing until Lorcan told me."

Tommy sighed. Dropped his hands between his knees. "Well, at least ye know. I really do think she's goin' tae finger ye for this so the Doyles aren't looked at."

"It doesn't take a rocket scientist tae work out it's them collectin' the drugs. Lorcan told me not tae go near that bridge because the garda are aware of what the Doyles are doin' —and that didn't come from me, all right? I don't want any trouble. Róisín's playin' a dangerous game, being involved wid them if the garda know about the drugs. She'll get burned, so she will. Just sit back and wait, let her create her own downfall."

Tommy rose. "What if she gets caught and it comes out that I had suspicions but never said anythin'? I could lose my job."

Ichabod shrugged. *"Then maybe ye should go higher than her cousin. Tell someone above his pay grade. If she's really undercover, then surely that person will already know about it. If they don't, there's your answer: she's dodgy. All I know is the Sullivans' deaths weren't on me."*

Tommy sighed. "Feck this shit."

Ichabod followed him to the back door, letting him out, and whispered, "How did ye get in, by the way?"

"That door was unlocked."

Ichabod frowned. He was sure he'd checked it before he'd settled down to sleep. "Good luck." He closed the door, twisted the key, and switched the outside light off, then the one for the kitchen.

A horrible thought occurred. What if one of the Doyles had picked the lock and planted that gun in here while he'd slept? He'd have to search the whole house. Get rid of it.

In the living room, he pondered what Tommy had said while opening drawers and the cupboards of the sideboard. Róisín had a job on her hands if she was going to fit him up. The Doyles would want to know why she'd put Ichabod's name forward when even they didn't want him arrested for it, or so they'd said. What was she doing, playing hero garda, letting the Doyles think she was in with them when really she wasn't? Or was it the other way around? It had to be the latter, otherwise she wouldn't be interested in Ichabod taking the blame so the light didn't shine on the Doyles—and her by association.

He put more kindling on the fire and stoked the flames, adding his jacket to the pyre. Then he took his phone out of his pocket. Before he searched the rest of the house, he needed to send a message. He replied to the last text Biffy had sent, the one telling him who the targets were.

ICHABOD: YOU MIGHT HAVE A PROBLEM.

BIFFY: IN WHAT WAY?

ICHABOD: JUST BEEN INFORMED THAT RÓISÍN IS AFTER ME FOR THE SHOOTING.

BIFFY: WHAT THE FECK?

ICHABOD: SO IT WASN'T ON YOUR ORDERS?

BIFFY: NO WAY. THANKS FOR THE HEADS-UP. DON'T CONTACT ME AGAIN.

Ichabod erased the messages. Paced. Wished he'd never come here. But it was done now, and Biffy would likely get hold of Róisín and tell her to back off—if she was in with the Doyles. If not, things could get a little tricky.

Chapter Fourteen

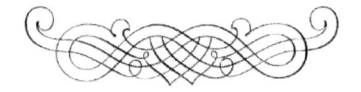

George, in his trusty Ruffian ginger beard and wig, Greg opting for his ZZ Top look with a red baseball cap, waited in their taxi on the main road near the airport. The lay-by, also occupied by a lorry, the driver kipping (George had got out and checked), wasn't close enough for him to see the long-stay car park. Thankfully, it was well outside the Congestion Charge and Low

Emission Zones, which meant their taxi wouldn't be picked up as having to pay any fees. They'd arrived by nine a.m., so plenty of time. Now they knew what the flight number was courtesy of Janine, they nosed at the Flightradar24 app periodically. The plane was in the air, but George couldn't stop himself from keep looking to make sure.

"If it's like Marleigh told Ichabod and David needs to take the goods to whoever he's working for first, then we might need to get nasty with them if it all goes wrong. Marleigh will be sitting in the bloody car and might get caught in the crossfire."

Greg nodded. "Call me suspicious but—"

"You, suspicious?" George laughed.

"Bog off. One of us needs to be overly cautious."

"Oi. I'm getting better at not trusting that people are telling us the truth."

"True, but it doesn't hurt to cover our backs. Anyway, as I was saying before I was rudely interrupted…"

"Fuck me, did you get up on the wrong side of the bed?"

"Let me *finish*, you fucking pleb."

George wanted to continue bugging him—it would pass the time nicely—but he sensed Greg was about to get a touch of Mad about him, one of George's alters. "Sorry. I'll shut up."

"Makes a change. So, what's your take on Marleigh offering that snippet?"

"What snippet?"

Greg tutted. "The one where David might have to drop the gear off. Christ, *you* were the one who brought it up. Have you got the memory of a goldfish today or what?"

George had already mulled that over. Not the goldfish bit but the drop-off scenario. "She could be stringing us a line. Making us follow her to wherever. Whoever employs David to collect drugs may want to do us some damage, and that's why she contacted us. To draw us to a place where we could be ambushed. Maybe she's in on the drugs thing. If we could have looked at her diary, we'd have known which way she really leans."

"Then we're on the same page. She was fine during the Goldie shit, I didn't have any reason to think she was off back then, but this time... I don't know. Marleigh and David could be a dodgy duo."

"Sounds like a crappy film title. Dodgy Duo Go Drug Trafficking."

Greg tsked again.

George told himself off and got back with the programme. "That's going to affect Ichabod. He likes her."

"Hmm." Greg folded his arms.

George leaned over, fishing in the glove box for a sweet.

"Sodding hell, bruv," Greg huffed. "Just ask me to get one for you. Your elbow's digging in my chuffing bollocks."

George sat upright. "Please can I have a lemon sherbet."

Greg took one out and handed it over. "There."

George unwrapped it. "But what if she's on the level?"

Greg sighed. "We'll soon find out when we listen in on the wire. She'd be stupid if she said she knows nothing about the drugs. David would ask her what she's guffing on about."

"Not if she shows him the wire so he knows to go along with it."

Greg grunted. "We should have given her a camera to put on the air vent on the dash. We could have watched her face for signs of lying."

"Too late now."

George crunched his sherbet lemon.

Greg sighed.

Chapter Fifteen

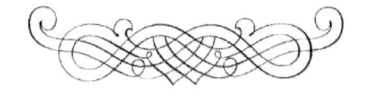

Ichabod had received a message before leaving Marleigh's. He'd been told to grill her—although he wouldn't be so harsh and actually grill—about whether this was a setup. Whatever had happened for the twins to think that, he didn't know, but he had to follow orders no matter what his feelings were towards the woman. Even if his dream came true and they got married, he'd still have to ask her things if he was told to. And keep certain Cardigan secrets.

She said no lies…

But she'd have to understand that sometimes, he'd have to tell them.

They were stuck in a traffic jam, although the snakes of cars on the dual carriageway moved forward, albeit slowly. His ankle ached from continually applying the brake. He could get off at the next junction but had to wait for the slip road to appear.

May as well get talkin' tae her now.

"I have tae ask ye somethin'. I'll say it straight out. The Brothers want tae know whether ye're spinnin' them a yarn. Are ye really in this wid David and he's been told tae ambush the twins?"

"*What?*" She glanced across at him, a sharp twist of her head. "I can't believe you've just asked me that."

"It wouldn't be unheard of. Husband-and-wife team."

"Oh, so I just wrote all that stuff in my diary—years ago—in case this sort of situation came up, did I?"

"Listen, I believe ye, but ye have tae understand I follow orders, and that's all I'm doin'. I'll let them know I trust ye. Goin' forward, there will be things I have tae say, things I can't tell ye, and ye need tae accept that and not badger me about it. Workin' for The Brothers has its own set of rules outside yours. Ye said no lies, and I get that, but ye must understand that what they say comes above what ye say."

"I do understand. David has secrets in his day job, too. I wouldn't expect you to spill Cardigan business. I'm not going to play the card that you're hiding things from me, because you've told me before we go forward. All I want is to know exactly where I stand, and you're giving it to me, so I can hardly moan about it later, can I."

"Thank ye."

The cars ahead had come to a stop, so he halted and held his phone low in his lap to send a quick text, conscious he could get done by the police for doing so if a camera caught him.

Ichabod: She's not dodgy, I'd put money on it.

He got a reply back quickly.

GG: Good. But we'll be on the lookout for anything odd anyway.

Ichabod: Agreed. Just in case.

GG: Yep. Fucking bored. You?

Ichabod: We're in a traffic jam. Thank God we left early.

GG: Is it likely to fuck things up?

Ichabod: No. GPS shows the red road warning stops not far ahead. It's green after that.

With no further response, he tucked the phone between his thighs.

"All sorted?" Marleigh asked. "Got the go-ahead to trust me?"

"Yep."

She rested her head back. "Want to tell me a story to pass the time?"

Ichabod nodded. But now the twins had put another grain of doubt in his mind, he couldn't help but wonder if she kept asking him about Ireland to stop him questioning her about the David thing.

Or does she want tae find out as much as she can about me so she can use it against me later?

Chapter Sixteen

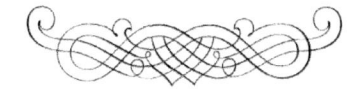

Ichabod left Granny's the next morning after eleven, as soon as Uncle Tadhg had come to sit with her for an hour or so. It was Saturday, and he wasn't sure what to do now, whether to go to the Fiddler's or back to the hotel to catch up on sleep, as he hadn't settled since Tommy had left during the night.

His curiosity got the better of him, and he walked to the pub. If there was any gossip to be had, Aoife would supply it, although her husband would be running the bar as it was daytime.

Ichabod stepped inside, relieved to see the landlady. He supposed she'd shown her face during the day shift because of the gossip. She'd want to pick it up so she could piece together what had happened to the Sullivans. Her eyes, red-rimmed, and her more-than-usual ruddy cheeks, told him she'd been crying. She'd been good friends with Caoimhe, so it was understandable.

He approached the bar and ordered the black stuff, adding a 'please' this time.

"Did ye hear the latest?" She pulled the Guinness pump, dark liquid pouring into the pint glass.

"I've heard nothin' since findin' out the Sullivans got shot."

"Well, so has Róisín. Dead as a bloody doornail, so she is."

It took a moment for Ichabod to process that, to get his emotions in order. Aoife would have already seen the shock in his expression, but that wasn't a bad thing.

"Err, what?"

"Someone broke into her house and shot her durin' the night." Aoife handed him his drink and produced the card reader.

Ichabod paid while she prattled on.

"Tommy discovered her early this mornin' when he went tae pick her up for work. Front door was on the jar, so he went in. Found her in the bedroom. Blood everywhere by all accounts, just what a Clancy deserves if ye ask me."

Ichabod sipped, needing the alcohol to steady his nerves. Had Biffy got someone to go and collect the gun straight after the shooting, before the garda had arrived at the farm? And how had the garda even known to go to the farm? Had someone phoned it in anonymously? The Doyle brothers' father, Sean, hadn't been in the pub last night. According to Auntie Niamh, who'd given Ichabod the lowdown on everyone when he'd first arrived, Sean was on bedrest, his wife, Erin, no longer on this earth to care for him, but being laid up wouldn't have stopped him from setting the garda in motion by using a burner phone. Or maybe the Sullivans had had a visitor who'd gone inside that office barn and seen the three men dead.

Or had someone been watching in the darkness to make sure Ichabod did the job? Otherwise, why tell him to leave the gun behind the tractor wheel if they weren't going to pick it up? That bit hadn't made sense at the time, because the garda would have found it, so unless it was a gun that belonged to someone they wanted to pin the murders on, surely Ichabod would have been told to dump it elsewhere. But if someone had been watching him...could Biffy have wanted that gun for future murders? Like Róisín's? Had he always planned to get rid of her, and Ichabod's message had sealed her fate earlier than intended? Should he feel guilty that she'd copped it?

No, because she was after framin' me.

"Are ye all right?" Aoife eyed him funny.

"Just shocked is all." He took another sip.

"Hmm. Tommy said the gun was left on the bed, so we'll soon see if it was the same one that killed the Sullivans. Did ye hear? They're dead, *not just shot."*

Ichabod nodded. "I'm that sorry for ye loss. Róisín and Tommy came tae speak tae me at Granny's last night and let me know. Wanted tae double-check what I was doin' before we came here."

"Pfft, ye already told them that, I heard ye."

"I know, but I suppose they have to be certain of their facts. I'm the only stranger in the village."

"Stranger? Away wid ye. Ye're one of us. And they should have spoken tae everyone else in here, too, yet they didn't."

Ichabod decided to stir the pot to take suspicion off the Doyles—only because if they were safe, so was he. "She mentioned some criminal gang in London, wondered if I knew them because I live there. To be sure, she was just doin' her job."

"Ye haven't got a murderous bone in ye body. What was she thinkin', basically accusin' ye?"

"I don't know, maybe she saw a link that isn't there. I just come here tae see my family, ye know that."

She narrowed her eyes. "What did ye talk about wid Lorcan?"

"He mentioned drugs bein' passed over on Burn Bridge."

"I see now. Róisín had the drug people on her radar, knew they came from London. Maybe wid the Sullivans bein' killed, the gang knew Lorcan had told Róisín about certain things goin' on. That's why they were taken out of the equation, even Róisín. They had tae be kept quiet."

Ichabod wouldn't disabuse her of that notion. It served a purpose for her to believe that and spread the hypothesis to others, but if Róisín wasn't bent, she'd have filed any reports about the drugs, so other officers would also know. Were their lives in danger, too?

"I think that's likely what happened," he said. "Nothin' else adds up."

She nodded. "I'm right, ye'll see. Sorry state of affairs either way. Not that I feel sorry for a Clancy or anythin'." She sucked on her bottom lip. "A member of that family wronged yours, so this is karma catchin' up wid them." She leaned over the bar, although it wasn't by much because of her height. She must be on tiptoes. *"This is how I think it went down. Lorcan saw the Doyles on that bridge. He phoned it in or he told Róisín on the quiet. The Doyles got wind, and now look. Once again, the garda won't be able tae prove it. Those brothers were in here from three o'clock, and old Sean couldn't have done anythin' as he's tae poorly at the minute. No, they'd have maybe got that London lot tae send someone over here and—"*

She stared at him, mouth open.

"See?" Ichabod said.

"Aye, now I get why Róisín thought it was ye. Silly girl. She couldn't be more wrong."

"I know nothin' about a drug gang, and like I told her, she was barkin' up the wrong tree. The first I heard of it was from Lorcan."

"It's all a bit too suspicious, but maybe this time the truth will come out. Those boys can't keep gettin' away wid it. When do ye go back?"

"Tomorrow, but I'm wonderin' whether I should stay another week so it doesn't seem like it's me who did it. Like I'm runnin' away."

"Probably a good idea. Anyway, it'll please ye family if ye stay on a while longer. Ye don't come for long enough, so..."

Aoife bustled off to serve someone else.

Her husband, Patrick, ambled over. He stood at around six feet, his steel-grey hair swept back. He jerked his head at his wife. "What's she been sayin'?"

"That Róisín is dead."

"Terrible business."

"It is." Ichabod explained Aoife's concocted theory. "So I think I should be stayin' another week. Even though I told Róisín and Tommy I'd be goin' back tomorrow, it's probably best for me tae stick around in case other garda need tae speak tae me."

"I wouldn't have thought they would, son. Everyone here knows ye're a good man, so they do, but ye do what ye think is best."

What was best was fecking off to London and hiding, keeping his head down, but if Róisín wasn't a bent garda and had passed her feelings on to her officer cousin before she'd clocked off for the night, it was possible Ichabod would get another visit.

Maybe Tommy would vouch for him, as would many other villagers. But Ichabod couldn't allow the garda to poke into his London life. To find out about the twins and his association with them. It would look bad.

All he could do was wait and see if someone from the garda came to ask follow-up questions. With Róisín dead, this had put a new spin on things. She'd asked him if he knew about the Directorates, and that could now be on file.

Thank God she'd queried him in front of Tommy so Ichabod had a witness who'd heard his answers, seen how confused he'd been.

Unless Tommy was the bent copper and had gone to Granny's to plant seeds…

The visit came later while Ichabod was at Auntie Niamh's eating his dinner. When Róisín's cousin, Shay Clancy, stepped into the kitchen where everyone sat around the table, the conversation stilled. Rowan glanced over at Ichabod, eyebrows raised. Ichabod shrugged in answer: No, I don't know what the feck he wants.

Niamh poked her head out from behind Shay where she stood in the hallway, then tapped his side to ask him to move so she could get past.

She retook her seat. "So what is it ye'll be wantin', Shay?"

Shay, all broad shoulders and severe features, gave a nod. "A quick word wid Ichabod here."

Ichabod smiled. "For sure, whatever ye want tae ask me, ye can do it in front of my family."

"Take a seat," Uncle Tadhg groused. "Ye're makin' the place look untidy. If ye want dinner, help yeself. Plates are over there." He pointed to that location then gestured to the food in serving dishes on the table. Sausage, mash, peas, and two boats of gravy.

How odd, for a Clancy to be offered dinner at an Ahearn's.

Shay collected a plate from the wall rack and sat at the end opposite Tadhg. "This is grand. Go raibh maith agat."

"No need tae be thankin' us," Tadhg said. "We're all friends — but only for tonight."

Ichabod sensed an underlying message there — that Tadhg was warning Shay to play nice, or maybe he was saying that the feud between the Ahearns and Clancys wouldn't be an issue while Shay was on garda business. Whatever, it was weird.

Shay filled his plate, relaxing somewhat. "What I've come tae say mustn't leave this room. I know there's a feud, but I've always trusted ye."

"Get on wid it," Tadhg snapped.

Shay sighed. *"As ye might have heard, Róisín is dead. I don't expect ye tae care because she's a Clancy but… She was shot at home."* He cut into a sausage, an obvious mask in place to hide his hurt. *"She was playin' an undercover role wid the Doyles, makin' out she was in wid them. Lorcan made us aware that somethin' was goin' down on Burn Bridge every Thursday—drugs being sold tae the Doyles."* He paused to eat a piece of sausage.

Niamh laid down her knife. *"I heard about that. Everybody has. Lorcan wasn't exactly keepin' it tae himself, although he did ask that nobody passed it on. But this is Caldraich. No one can stop themselves from twitterin' behind their hands. I told him tae stop spreadin' the word, that if it* was *the Doyles he'd seen and they found out what he'd been sayin', they'd go for him. Shut him up."*

"Why didn't anyone tell me or Róisín?" Shay asked.

Niamh picked up her knife and fork. Jabbed the knife at him. *"One, ye're garda, and no one wants the hassle. Two, ye're Clancys—again, no one wants the hassle. And three, no one would want the Doyles findin' out what's been said, and they would if ye went up tae them and asked them outright."*

Shay nodded. "Fair enough. I wanted tae tell ye, Ichabod, that I'm not lookin' at ye for the Sullivans' deaths. Róisín had it in her head ye'd come over from London tae do the job. I spoke tae her last night after her shift ended. Told her ye'd never gun that family down in cold blood. That the London gang is bein' tracked by the Met and it's all in hand. She went off half-cocked sometimes, got tunnel vision. Sadly, whoever killed her must have found out she was diggin' deep and they took exception tae it. Tommy has said ye were at Granny Maeve's all night so it couldn't have been ye who killed her."

"What was he doin'?" Ichabod asked. "Watchin' me?"

"He went back to ye granny's after he'd come tae the station once he'd spoken tae ye. He told my senior officer, passed on his suspicions about Róisín. I was called in, and we had tae explain tae Tommy what was goin' on, that Róisín wasn't bent."

Ichabod frowned. "But why would I need tae be watched?"

"In case Róisín let it slip tae the Doyles that she thought ye'd killed the Sullivans. She'd have thought she was doin' the right thing by tellin' them that. She'd have wanted tae gauge their reactions as tae whether they were behind it. If she said she suspected it was ye,

then they'd have relaxed. Maybe tripped up later down the line."

"So she could have used my name tae get a result?" Ichabod shook his head. *"Of all the dangerous, stupid things tae do."*

He recalled what Lorcan had said on the night of the murders. That the police were going to watch Burn Bridge on Thursday. But he couldn't repeat it, because Tommy had said Shay was dodgy. Could he be trusted?

"I can see why she did that, but I don't appreciate bein' dragged into somethin' that's got nothin' tae do wid me."

"This is why I'm here." Shay smiled sadly. *"I need tae put this right. I might turn the other way from time tae time, but not on somethin' as big as this. She said ye're goin' back tae London tomorrow."*

"Yep, but I was thinkin' of stayin' another week."

"Then do that. If it's as we suspect, the Directorates might come after ye there. Wait until we've apprehended the Doyles."

Ichabod swallowed some mash. *"The Doyles wouldn't risk blurtin' that out, they'll worry about repercussions in prison, so when I do go back tae London, if Róisín's dropped my name in it, that gang might come after me anyway."*

"The Met are closin' in. They'll be followin' those gang members who are comin' here to drop off drugs on Thursday. While they're bein' caught here, the Met will be roundin' up the ones in London."

Ichabod thought of the twins. Whether they'd be dragged into this if any of the Cardigan drug pushers bought supplies from the Directorates, whoever the feck they were. George and Greg allowed the sale of drugs so long as protection money was paid, so they were in the loop somewhere and could find themselves right in the shite.

"Where are the Directorates based?" he asked.

"North London."

He hid his relief. That meant it was another Estate leader's problem. "Then that's nowhere near me. I'm East End."

Shay shrugged. "Still, isn't it better that ye're here rather than there for now?"

"I'm more of a target here. The Doyles could pick me off before I get a chance tae go back if Róisín has dropped my name tae them. In London, I have places where I can hide out until this is over."

The Brothers would help him out there.

"Then go tae London tomorrow. Make sure ye don't come out of hidin' until I give ye the word. We'll swap numbers. I'll contact ye."

As though they hadn't just spoken about all this, the chatter moved on to other things. How Shay felt about losing his cousin, when she'd be allowed a funeral, Niamh adding how the Ahearns would shun the service, staying away to make a point that even in death, her family wouldn't mourn the passing of a Clancy.

"What's the craic on that?" Ichabod asked. "The feud."

Everyone went silent, although Rowan seemed interested to know the answer, too.

"No one talks about that," Niamh said.

Well, that put an end tae that, didn't it?

Chapter Seventeen

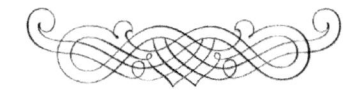

David had got through airport security and now waited by the luggage carousel for his two cases. The second one had a special compartment that sealed the drugs away from the clothing and souvenirs packed in there. How the Brazilian suppliers managed to get it into the compartment every time without any drug scent or transference being picked up he didn't know and had never asked. Not to mention the weight, although he paid extra for that to cover for the ornaments he always bought home and gave to his mother. All the trips he'd come back from before had seen him sailing through, his luggage never opened.

He didn't understand it, never had. Surely there were scanners that could see the packages of cocaine inside. Or was there some kind of impenetrable cover that blocked out the shape of the drug bricks? Or, which was more likely, people at both airports worked for the same man as David. That would be why the boss insisted on picking the flight times himself so someone was on shift to let the case sail through.

The boss went by the name of Charlie Weed, a bloody ridiculous moniker, a piss-take, the bloke always in a balaclava whenever David had meetings with him. However the job was done, it had worked so far, but he wondered, on every single trip, whether today would be the day his cases never appeared and he was pulled out of the security queue.

His break from doing this, back when he'd first started getting serious with Marleigh, had been a reprieve from the anxiety that had gripped his stomach on the drug runs. He'd promised himself he wouldn't do it again, not now he was married and had a bloody good job that paid so well.

The phone call three years ago had changed that.

Mr Weed had rung him out of the blue, asking him to think about becoming one of the members of his core team again. While David earned a lot of money in his day job, and he'd told Marleigh she could spend whatever she liked, that was more outlay than he'd expected. Her clothing bill alone was extortionate, and his credit cards only had so much available funds on them. He guessed she was bored, shopping an addiction. The lure of drug money had snagged him once again, and that had meant keeping secrets from his wife.

Not to mention the young, pretty brunette he stayed with while in Brazil.

David had put his hand up in a meeting at work, offering to do some face-to-face negotiations abroad, his excuse being that he needed more strings to his bow. Harry had agreed without question. It gave David the cover he needed, and he'd told Marleigh his role had expanded. She wasn't happy but had soon got used to it. He took her with him on the legitimate travel to Vegas but not the Brazil runs, obviously. Mr Weed had insisted he used his real passport as the fakes these days could be spotted so easily, and that added to the burden.

He spotted his cases and moved forward to grab them. Hauling them off the conveyor belt, he casually glanced around to check for any security watching him. All appeared fine, so he pushed his luggage towards the exit, not stopping to put the bag containing the duty-free perfume for his mother in the smaller case.

He *had* to get out of there.

The fresh air hit him along with the release of anxiety, his legs going a tad wobbly. He'd done it. He was free on English soil yet again, but how long would his luck last? He continued on with other commuters and holidaymakers towards the long-stay car park, reminding himself of his next steps. He had to drive to the lock-up and hand the large case over to Mr Weed who'd then distribute the drugs to dealers in the East End. Naughty of him, especially when The Brothers ran Cardigan and they'd go apeshit if they found out. But Mr Weed liked danger and didn't want drugs on his home turf.

David walked across the car park, thinking about how he'd face Marleigh today. How he'd deal with her tears. Her snide words. She'd still be angry that he'd been away for Christmas. She'd told him to lie if his mother rang him, saying they were spending the break quietly at home. She'd never been one to show others that their marriage wasn't like it used to be.

David had never acknowledged that whenever she'd spoken to him about it. His mind had been elsewhere. Marleigh was a heavy ball and chain around his neck now, one he wished he could rip off. His feelings towards her were dead, had been for some time, yet he'd still maintained the charade, coming home and pretending everything was all right. Mainly because he'd wanted to keep the house, except his wife was still in it, and perhaps because he didn't have the bottle back then to call it a day with her. His mother wouldn't be pleased, she adored his wife. He'd been persuaded to let their home go, though. In order to have what he wanted, he'd have to. That was one of the stipulations of starting his new life.

He'd say he missed her, that woman he'd waited down the end of the aisle for, but he didn't. He'd changed. She'd changed. They'd become so different. She was suspicious when he first came home from an airport run, giving him weird glances, asking him questions as if to trip him up. She soon settled down, though, back into their regular pattern, and he did, too, making out all was well and he wasn't missing his Brazilian beauty.

If only he hadn't said yes to Mr Weed, then he'd still be happy with Marleigh.

But then he wouldn't have met Janaína. Would never have had baby Felipe.

Christ.

He'd promised Janaína he'd end it with Marleigh this time. Move out, leaving her the house and everything in it. Start again so Janaína and Felipe could come to live in the UK. *That* part he wasn't sure on. Wouldn't it be rubbing it in Marleigh's face if they all bumped into each other in town? He'd have to deal with the histrionics.

Their altercation before he'd left this time still played on his mind. How could he tell her he'd wanted to spend his son's first Christmas with him? He couldn't, so he'd come up with some bullshit excuse about clients who didn't celebrate Christmas, men who were being awkward and wanted their meeting over the festive season. Instead, he'd spent it with his mistress and her family, swallowed up by their domineering presence. If he didn't love Janaína so much, he'd have bowed out by now. Her family meant everything to her. He worried he was a close second. Would never be her sole reason for living.

He swore Marleigh suspected something was going on. She'd brought up the subject of a story on Mumsnet where a man had a secret family. The Original Poster had queried whether she was…what was the acronym? AIBU, that was it. Am I Being Unreasonable? The OP had gone on to ask whether she was justified in being angry that her husband had another partner and four children in Sussex where he supposedly worked every other week. He'd been alternating his time between both women. The reason she'd asked if she was justified was because the husband had said she wasn't.

David had laughed, saying some men were such arseholes, weren't they? Yet all the while, he was one of them. The shock of her being so close to the truth had sent his cheeks hot, and he'd had to leave the room before she'd seen them.

He couldn't keep doing this. Lying.

His love for Janaína transcended anything he'd ever felt for his wife. Now he knew what true love was, he realised he should never have married Marleigh. And it *was* true love, otherwise he wouldn't put up with Janaína's family. After telling Marleigh, he had to face his mother. It wasn't going to go down well. She'd take Marleigh's side.

It's all a bit of a mess, really.

He approached the car and frowned. Someone sat in the passenger seat.

Oh Jesus, is that Marleigh? What the fuck is she doing here? She must have used the spare key to get in.

He slapped on a smile to cover his intense, body-freezing shock and ducked to see her through the driver's-side window, his stomach churning. He waved. Gestured that he'd put the cases in the boot, his hand movement overexaggerated. God, had she spotted Mum's duty-free bag swinging on his wrist? Would she think he'd bought *her* a present? He hadn't done so this time, not wanting to confuse her with a gift when he was about to tell her it was over. That would be *too* cruel on top of everything else.

He frowned. Why hadn't she got out to greet him with one of her usual suffocating hugs? He used to appreciate those, the proof she'd missed him, but now he hated them.

They made him feel guilty, and he was always conscious she'd smell Janaína's perfume. Maybe she already had and was playing a game, waiting for the perfect moment to catch him out. To mention it. Gauge his reaction.

He stowed the cases, hiding behind the lid of the boot to compose himself for a moment. What was she doing here? How had she got here? Why hadn't she waited until he'd arrived home? And more importantly, how had she found out what flight he was on? He never disclosed those details to her and always lied about his destination, saying he was elsewhere.

He shut the lid and took a deep breath. Told himself he could do this. Got in the passenger seat. He'd have to make up some excuse as to why he needed to go to the lock-up. He couldn't risk having the drugs in his car at home. Plus, Mr Weed would already be waiting for him. To not turn up would bring a whole load of trouble down on his head. Seat belt on, he leaned over to kiss her cheek. She didn't smell like Janaína, and it brought on a pang of longing for the other woman.

"Well, this is a surprise," he said.

"I thought it might be." She sounded in a mood.

God.

He turned the engine on and manoeuvred out of the space. "What brought you here? Has something serious happened? To my mum?"

"No, I just thought I'd make the welcome home arrive sooner."

Home. It wouldn't be his anymore, but he'd come to terms with that. While away, he'd already sourced a swanky flat in Wapping for himself, Janaína, and their son. It came furnished, so that was a bonus. He'd planned to nip to collect the keys from the landlord after seeing Mr Weed, but Marleigh had complicated things.

He got on the road, heading in the direction of the lock-up, a bit worried; Marleigh hadn't spoken for a while, and that was never a good sign.

"Something wrong?" he asked.

"Just wondering why we're going this way."

"Oh, I need to deliver something to Harry."

"What's that, the drugs?"

His foot pressed on the brake in his terror, his skin going cold all over. He swerved dangerously, then righted the wheel, a chorus of honking horns, several drivers telling him off. "What?"

"I found the ledger."

"What ledger?"

"Don't act as if I'm stupid. In your private safe. The one with my birthdate as the unlock code."

She'd gone *snooping*? Shit a fucking brick. Should he admit it? Tell her she'd bought things with the proceeds of illegal money, like the outfit she had on now? Make her feel implicated enough that she'd keep her stupid mouth shut? Use it as an excuse to leave her instead of confessing he had a mistress and little boy abroad? "I can explain."

"Go on then. Let's see what gem you come up with."

From the corner of his eye, he caught her folding her arms. He was in for a rough ride. "Look, there's this man called Mr Weed…"

"Oh, *please*." She laughed. "Do you think I'm that naïve?"

"I'm serious, that's what I know him as. I used to work for him before we met, when I was a teenager. I stopped when I met you, then he got hold of me again."

"Three years ago by any chance?"

He clenched his teeth. "If you've seen the ledger, then you know it is."

"Actually, I was going by when you changed."

He was going to have to be a bastard and blame it on her, but if it meant he made her hate him, made her let him go without *too* much hassle, then it would be worth it. "Right, well… I…I don't know what else to say except you forced me into it."

"*Me*?"

"Yes, all that spending. I couldn't keep up." He didn't even feel bad for putting this all at her door. He was in a tight spot, determined to get out of it with the least amount of shrapnel in his heart and mind as possible. To maintain having an affair had taught him something—that he was a good liar.

She sighed. "Ah, there's a new Mr in the equation as well, then. I should have known."

"What do you mean?"

"Mr Gaslighter. Make the good little woman think it's all her fault so she keeps it to herself. Give me a break. So are we on the way to see Mr Weed now, not Harry? Of course we are. Harry doesn't even live this way. We're going to Canning Town, right?"

How did she know? Or was it just a guess because of the direction they were going in? "Yes. I'll drop the…the stuff off, then we can talk about it at home."

"Why, so it gives you time to perfect your story?"

He clamped his mouth shut. He wasn't going to be drawn into an argument while driving. But when they got home, he'd let her have the lot. Definitely blame her for him falling into Janaína's arms, see how she liked *that*.

Chapter Eighteen

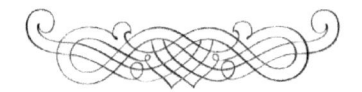

Marleigh fumed. How *dare* he swing this round so it was her fault? All she'd ever done was be there for him, keeping his house pristine and herself looking perfect so he didn't need to go elsewhere. Entertaining his mother on her visits while he was away. Limiting how often she left the house while he was home. She'd built her life around *his* calendar, forgoing what *she*

wanted. A more present husband. Someone she still loved. Yes, she'd homed in on him at the very beginning, recognising that he could provide for her, and that was wrong, she knew that now, but did that mean she deserved *this*? To be expected to shut up and put up when she knew he was breaking the law?

No.

Him saying they would talk about this at home was typical of David these days. He'd want to get his ducks in a row. God, all those times she'd pretended they were the perfect couple when they weren't, just to save face. All because of how it would appear to other people. She wished she hadn't bothered. Wished she'd never met him.

But if she hadn't, she wouldn't have seen that refugee in the window and contacted the twins. She wouldn't have met Ichabod.

Maybe life had directed her exactly where she was supposed to go. Her path with David had led her to a charming Irishman, someone she could see herself happy with, despite everything he'd done and all he would do in the future. Despite frowns and queries from her family and friends.

None of that mattered. Being happy did.

Why had it taken her so long to realise that?

She checked the wing mirror. The black cab still followed.

David swerved down a side road. Skinny terraced houses with blank-stare windows gave no sign of life inside. People were probably at work, luckily living their lives oblivious to what she was going through. Halfway down, he turned into a single-car lane between two homes that led to an area similar to a car park. A row of five lock-ups faced her, with roller fronts and metal doors. A black SUV with a vanity plate drew her eye, two men inside it. David parked next to it and got out, as did the men.

Balaclavas covered their faces.

Marleigh's stomach rolled over, and she whispered for the wire, "Two men are here. Faces covered. They're going into the middle lock-up. David's going to the boot for the case."

She sat in silence while he took it out and wheeled it to the lock-up door, disappearing inside. Letting out an unsteady breath, she hoped the twins had parked somewhere close and had left the taxi to come here and keep an eye on her.

She needn't have worried. Movement to the right, at the side of the last lock-up. A man in black, face also covered, held up one hand using the 'okay' sign. He was as tall as George and just as big, so perhaps it was him.

She relaxed and, to take her mind off the tangle her life had become, she thought back over more of Ichabod's story.

Chapter Nineteen

While his aunt and uncle cleared up after dinner, insisting they didn't need any help, Ichabod sat with Rowan in the living room. Despite them living so far away from each other as they'd grown up, and Rowan being five years younger, they were still close, having kept in touch via phone, emails, and then WhatsApp messages. Rowan had the look about him that he had something on his mind, and Ichabod braced himself. Would, or should, he answer anything his cousin asked? Yes, he could trust him, but he'd promised himself he wouldn't involve family in this. Maybe he should see how the conversation went first and go with his gut.

"What do ye really do in London?" *Rowan glanced at the door, perhaps checking if it was shut properly. He clearly had something he wanted to ask that he didn't want his parents to know about.*

Ichabod narrowed his eyes and spoke quietly, his suspicion gene flaring. Not that he thought Rowan would grass him up for anything, but still, it was odd for him to ask, now, when he hadn't before. "Why do ye need tae know?"

"Because ye asked Shay where the Directorates are based. Why would that matter tae ye if ye don't even know who they are?"

Ichabod sighed. "Ye really don't want tae know."

"I do."

Was it time to tell all? To reveal who he'd really become as an adult? That he wasn't a labourer or brickie? "Ye can't tell anyone."

Rowan glared at him. "What do ye take me for? When have I ever blabbed anythin' ye've told me?"

"It's worse than anythin' ye'd likely imagine."

Rowan nodded. "Thought so. Ye've not seemed the same for a while."

Ichabod would start with London, see how that panned out first. If he thought Rowan could handle the truth about the Sullivans, then he might well confess to that, too. Just that decision alone took some of the weight off his shoulders. He hadn't realised how much pressure he'd been under.

"I work for two men. Twins. They run an Estate."

Eyes wide, Rowan reared his head back in alarm. "As in a proper Estate? Like the ones I've seen on the news?"

Ichabod picked at a fingernail. "Yeah."

"Jaysus." Rowan sat forward. "I'd never have had ye pegged as a criminal — that's what ye're sayin' ye are, aren't ye?"

"Somethin' like that."

"How did ye get involved?"

Ichabod tripped out a gruff laugh. "Too long a story, but let's just say I was skint and took the best option open tae me at the time. I don't regret it. I've got a purpose now. I belong tae somethin' much bigger than myself. A family."

"Are ye happy tae do it?"

Was he? "Yep."

"And just what is it ye do?"

"I follow people. Watch them. Beat a few up if that's what's called for. I'm a foot soldier, but I want tae climb the ranks. Be someone more important within the organisation. Earn more money and get a bigger place."

Rowan's eyebrows rose. "What do ye mean, more important?"

"A proper heavy."

Rowan laughed. "Wid that scrawny arse of yours? Away wid ye."

"What? I could go tae the gym, beef myself up. I'm already a black belt in martial arts."

"Ye kept that quiet." Rowan gazed off, as though gearing himself up to ask another question.

Ichabod stared at the coffee table so his cousin didn't feel so exposed—being under the spotlight when you had something important to say made for discomfort. He should know, he'd just felt like it. "Come on, out wid it. I know there's somethin' else ye want tae say."

Rowan couldn't look more bewildered if he tried. What the hell was going on with him?

"Don't shout at me, all right?"

"I can't promise I won't."

Rowan took a deep breath. "Did ye kill the Sullivans?"

Bollocks. Truth or lie? *"I don't want tae bring ye into anythin'."*

"I already am because ye've basically admitted it by not sayin' 'no'. So did ye?"

"Depends what ye'd do wid the information if I said yes."

"Shit, man. Were ye sent by the Directorates?"

"Nah, but if I was, I'd still have done it because it would likely have been a favour for the twins regardin' another leader. They'd have paid me a good wedge that I wouldn't have turned down."

"Why did ye do it?"

Ichabod glanced up. *"Because if I didn't, Granny would be dead."*

Rowan's face paled. *"Oh. Feck."*

"Yeah, feck." Ichabod stretched his legs out. *"She's family, so I had tae save her. There was no question. No hesitation."*

"I'd have done the same, though I'd have been brickin' it. I can't imagine how ye felt. There was a gun. Where did ye get it?"

"They gave it tae me. The people who asked me tae do it."

"Who was it?"

"Ye don't need tae ask that. Isn't it obvious?"

"The feckin' Doyles." Rowan let out a long, unsteady breath.

"Yeah, they basically abducted me on Thursday, just so ye know. Put a stinkin' bag over my head. I didn't have a choice in this. They took me somewhere, don't know where, then told me what they wanted me tae do. After that, they dumped me on Corduroy Road."

"So Róisín was right about ye, just not for the correct reason."

"Hmm."

"Did ye end her?"

"No, I can swear on that. But I might have had somethin' tae do wid the outcome."

"Like what?"

"I let Biffy know she was sniffin' around."

"That's not like ye. Don't ye feel bad?"

Ichabod shook his head. *"No, she was comin' for me, and she's a Clancy. I've learned a lot in London. It's a dog-eat-dog world."*

"Are there any jobs for me in London?"

The sudden change of subject gave Ichabod a jolt. *"Plenty."*

"Wid your bosses?"

"Yep."

"Could ye put in a word for me?"

"Why? I thought ye said ye'd stay in Caldraich forever, that ye never wanted tae leave. What's changed?"

Rowan fiddled with his fingers. Glanced at the door again. "I was seein' a Clancy."

That was brave. And stupid. "Was?"

"Aye. My mammy found out and told me tae nip it in the bud before anyone heard about it. What the feck went on wid us and that lot?"

"Did ye not hear me ask at the table? I know ye did, so why say that?"

"It was rhetorical."

Ichabod grinned. "Big word for an eejit like ye."

"Feck off."

They laughed but sobered quickly.

"She's pregnant," Rowan said. "The Clancy."

"Shite."

"She's off tae England tae get rid of it on Monday so no one around here catches on. Ye know what they're like. Eyes like those feckin' eagles. One whiff that she's carryin', and the whole village will be speculatin', spreadin' gossip."

"She didn't want tae marry ye?"

"She did, but I'm Ahearn and she's Clancy. We shouldn't have started anythin' in the first place. Even though they haven't spoken for years, my mammy told

her mammy, and it all went wrong. We were banned from seein' each other. I don't get it."

"Do ye love her?"

Rowan shrugged. "Maybe."

"Either ye do or ye don't. Stop feckin' about and just tell me."

"Yeah, I love her."

"Then ask her tae run away wid ye."

"She won't leave Caldraich. I've already suggested it."

"So ye're okay wid her goin' off wid someone else in the village, right under ye nose? Because she will eventually."

"When she does, I'll come tae London. That's why I asked about jobs, so I have somethin' in the pipeline."

"Why not come back wid me tomorrow? It'll only be torture otherwise."

"Because I was hopin' someone would tell us why we can't be together, then we can make a fix around it or understand why it isn't possible."

"Ye know what these feuds are like amongst the villagers. They last for centuries."

"This one's bullshit because it's messin' wid my life."

Ichabod sucked in a big breath. Let it out. "I'm goin' tae tell ye the bald truth. If she proper loved ye, she'd leave, no matter what. She wouldn't get rid of the baby. She'd want tae go wid ye, make a home somewhere else. And why *doesn't she want it?"*

Rowan inhaled through his nostrils. "I've already thought of that. I'm stayin' until I know what happened in the past, and if I agree wid why we can't be together, then I'll make myself scarce."

"Fine, but I expect she'd have copped off with someone else by the time ye know the truth. Shall we go for a drink?"

Rowan nodded and stood. Smoothed his shirt fronts. "May as well. It's not like I've got a girlfriend tae go and see anymore, is it."

In the Fiddler's, Ichabod stood at the bar near Patrick while Aoife worked behind it. Rowan was off talking to someone or other, most definitely not a Clancy, but probably trying to find a man or woman who'd tell him the story.

Ichabod planned to do the same with Patrick. "Why is everyone so quiet about what happened between the Ahearns and Clancys?"

"Nasty business."

"Which was?"

Patrick shook his head. "I have no idea, and even if I did, I wouldn't repeat it. Aoife would have my guts for garters. Ask Niamh or Tadhg. It's the best-kept secret in Northern Ireland, and ye'll only be told if ye promise never tae mention it tae anyone else. Feuds are secret things. Why do ye want tae know?"

Ichabod shrugged. "Aoife being overly short with Róisín tugged at my curiosity."

"That killed the cat."

"Supposedly."

Patrick eyed him. "Ye don't want it tae kill ye, do ye?"

"It's that bad?"

"Yep. The whispers say that if anyone breathes a word out loud, if what happened gets out, people will come. Certain Ahearns and Clancys will die."

"Bloody hell…"

"Hmm. Makes me glad I don't know the ins and outs." Patrick ambled off, through the doorway to the toilets.

A few seconds later, Biffy followed him.

This instance of curiosity also might get him killed, but Ichabod went after them anyway, unable to stop himself. His training with the twins, to chase leads, was now ingrained in him. In the corridor, he contemplated going into the men's and seeing if he could catch them in conversation while they had a piss, but a door at the end flapped in the wind, the one that led to the back yard. He walked towards it, Patrick's voice carrying inside.

Standing against the wall so if the door opened inwards it would shield him from view, Ichabod listened.

"So Róisín was down tae ye," Patrick said.

"Yeah. She would have fecked everythin' up," Biffy replied.

"How did ye find out she would've done that?"

Ichabod held his breath in case his name was mentioned.

A snort. "I have ways and means, ye know that. Little grasses who tell me what's goin' on. All I need tae know is whether ye can go on a holiday wid the packages. Without Aoife."

"When?"

"Tomorrow. I've got a weird feelin' that somethin's about tae go down, so I want the goods moved, taken well out of Caldraich."

"Are ye cancellin' the next drop?"

"No. I've set up a new exchange place, Folly Courtyard, four a.m. on Thursday. The garda are all over the farm in their white suits, and they might be *for a while. I can't risk them spottin' anythin' goin' on at the bridge."*

"But how will I collect it if I'm away?"

"Ye'll only be gone long enough tae take the goods tae the safe place. Ye'll go tae Limerick, a four-hour drive. We have men there who'll take it off ye hands. Ye'll stay there until I tell ye tae come back."

"I'm tryin' tae think of an excuse to tell Aoife as tae why I'm goin' away."

"Start an argument. Do what it takes so ye can storm out, but make sure the stuff's in suitcases well before that. We can't risk her followin' ye around, shoutin' the odds, seein' what ye're packin'. Ye know what she gets like when her dander's up."

"Don't I know it. Okay, I'll pack it all up now, ready."

"I'll send ye the address in Limerick. Leave later tonight, after the pub's shut."

"When I do the Folly exchange, do I then need tae move the new goods tae Limerick?"

"No, John's off tae Cork wid his girlfriend on Friday next week. He can deal wid it, take a detour tae Limerick."

Ichabod had heard enough. He rushed off to the toilet — he didn't think he'd make it to the other end of the corridor in time before they came back in. He stood in a cubicle, picking over what he'd heard. It was obvious Patrick was well in with the Doyles and had been for some time.

I'd never have guessed.

Footsteps. The door of the next cubicle slamming.

Ichabod flushed the loo and washed his hands, the devil inside telling him to hang around to see who emerged. Worry gripped him. What if Alastar or John had seen him following Patrick and Biffy? The Doyle brothers were usually always together, but he couldn't remember if the other two had been in the bar. Maybe he'd get lucky and they weren't.

The other toilet flushed, and the door opened.

Biffy strode out. "Still in town?"

"I go back tomorrow."

"Make sure ye do."

Ichabod had to know for sure. "Róisín?"

"Yep, thanks tae ye. I'm in ye debt."

That was a big thing, coming from Biffy.

Ichabod decided to give him more information, extra insurance to keep the Doyles off his back, although that might not matter with what he planned to do later. "She played ye. She wasn't in wid ye, she was doin' it for the garda."

"Bitch. How did ye find out?"

"Shay came for dinner at Niamh's tonight."

"A Clancy having dinner wid the Ahearns? Feck me."

"He'd come on police business tae speak tae me."

"What about?"

"Whether I knew about the drugs. He told us tae keep what he said tae ourselves. I think he knows ye killed her, so be careful."

Biffy glanced across at him. "Why are ye tellin' me this? It's not like we ever got on, and we abducted ye, for feck's sake."

Ichabod smiled. "Ye know damn well why. It's simple. I want my granny left alone. All of my family."

Biffy gave a curt nod. "Done."

He walked out.

Ichabod sighed in relief, but he'd do a bit more shit-stirring to ensure the Doyles never touched an Ahearn because they'd hopefully be in prison. He walked into the bar, noted John and Alastar weren't in, and asked someone for a cigarette and matches, going outside to fake smoke it. He strode far enough away from the pub that he wouldn't be overheard and rang Shay.

"Promise me ye won't drop my name into this," he said, voice low.

"I won't."

"Got tae be quick in case someone comes outside. I'm at the pub."

"Go on..."

"Patrick's in with the Doyles."

"Shite. Which Patrick?"

"Gallagher. He's the one who stores the drugs. He's takin' them tae Limerick tonight."

"How do ye know this?"

"I overheard him talkin' tae Biffy in the yard. The drugs won't be dropped off at the bridge on Thursday. It's now Folly Courtyard, four a.m. Sounds like Patrick's used to do the exchange sometimes, as he's got tae be back from Limerick in time tae collect at the Folly. Those drugs will be taken tae Limerick next Friday by John."

"Go raibh maith agat."

Ichabod cut the call. Deleted the call log. Brought up a new message for the twins.

ICHABOD: YOU MIGHT WANT TO WARN WHOEVER RUNS AN ESTATE IN NORTH LONDON THAT THE MET ARE ONTO WHOEVER THE DIRECTORATES ARE.

GG: HOW THE FUCK DO YOU KNOW STUFF LIKE THAT WHEN YOU'RE OVER THERE?

ICHABOD: IT'S LINKED TO A FAMILY HERE CALLED THE DOYLES. SHIT HAS GONE DOWN. THE INFO HASN'T COME FROM ME, ALL RIGHT? I CAN'T RISK IT GETTING BACK THAT I GRASSED.

GG: CHEERS.

Ichabod dropped the cigarette and matches in a bush and went into the pub.

Rowan stood by the bar, glum as anything.

"What's up wid ye?" Ichabod whispered. "Did ye find out what the feud is?"

"No bastard will tell me."

"Come tae London wid me anyway."

"No, if there's a chance for me and…and the woman I was seeing, I want tae take it."

Ichabod held back a snort. There was no way he'd *let a woman get to* him *like that. Girls sent you daft.*

Chapter Twenty

Greg crept out from the side of the lock-up and moved quietly towards the SUV. He ignored Marleigh's alarmed look and went to stand behind the black vehicle. He stared at the number plate, and his guts churned.

What the fucking hell is he doing here?

This changed everything. He contemplated abandoning the mission if this bloke was involved. The bringing in of drugs could all be solved with a quick, amicable visit now. They'd find out whether any of the gear made it to Cardigan, and if they were assured it didn't, he and George would back off.

Not from David, though. That man had lied to Marleigh. Their private investigator, Mason, had got back to them while they'd sat in the lay-by. David had a regular monthly payment of four thousand pounds from his bank to a Miss Janaína Pereira's account. Upon further foraging into the Brazilian woman, Mason had discovered she had a son, six-month-old Felipe. That was as far as he'd got and had promised to dig further.

Greg retreated, going back down the side of the lock-up. George, currently sitting in the taxi in the street, might well go ballistic when Greg told him what the number plate was. In fact, 'might' didn't come into it. Mad George would come out. All hell would break loose.

Two of their men waited, high hedges intruding into the cramped space.

"Wait here," Greg whispered. "Only make a move when they leave. Contact us if things go tits up. Keep an eye on Marleigh."

Greg tromped down the passageway and turned left. Walked behind the lock-ups until he reached a footpath between houses. He made it back to the taxi and got in.

"You'll never guess who Mr Weed is," he said.

"Who?"

Greg told him.

George scowled his Mad scowl. "We'll fucking kill him."

Chapter Twenty-One

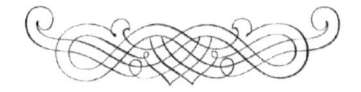

Ichabod paced the hallway in Marleigh's house, his car parked down the road, far enough away from the property for David not to twig anything was going on. Ichabod had arranged with Marleigh for her to encourage her husband to park in the garage, then go into the living room. Ichabod would let the twins in. David would be marched into the garage and bundled into his own car boot.

Ichabod's phone beeped, and he jumped, his nerves strung tight.

GG: News just in. The man D works for, we know him.

Ichabod: Shite. Will it complicate things?

GG: Not D's disposal, no.

Ichabod: Anything I can do to help with the man?

GG: Definitely not, but cheers for the offer.

Ichabod: Is everything still going to plan?

GG: Yep. We'll deal with the drug boss separately.

Ichabod stared at the screen. There was nothing else for him to say.

Another bleep.

GG: How much do you want to kill D?

Ichabod: Like you wouldn't believe.

GG: Well, add this to your list of hates. He's got a bird and possible kid in Brazil.

Ichabod's heart lost several beats. So Marleigh had been right. Mammy had mentioned once or twice that a woman's intuition was usually always spot-on. The thought of Marleigh finding out this information wrenched his emotions.

Poor cow.

Another message came through.

GG: ON THE MOVE. SEE YOU SHORTLY.

A deep breath, and Ichabod backed into the kitchen, wedging himself beside the American fridge-freezer, pulling the kitchen door towards him so it shielded him from view. It reminded him of hiding when Patrick had spoken to Biffy in the yard. It was best to hide again here. Just in case David took it upon himself to ignore his wife and sit in this room.

If he did, Ninja Ichabod would be waiting.

Chapter Twenty-Two

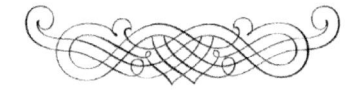

Back in London, on the day of the drug delivery at Folly, Ichabod sat with a twin either side of him, opposite Solly Moss, one of the North London leaders. While Ichabod had his bosses with him, it still didn't stop him from shitting his kecks. When he'd first followed Solly's skinny, butler-like assistant down a set of cellar stairs he'd expected the worst, but once

he'd got to the bottom, his fears had subsided. No creepy, damp-riddled walls, no fusty smell.

Instead, a short hallway leading to darkness and what amounted to a small office in front of him, although it only took up one section of what must otherwise be a large space beneath the mansion-type house. Clearly, stud walls had been put up to create this room. It had a closed-in feel to it, inciting claustrophobia, all dark-green walls, grey file boxes on tall bookcases to the right and left, and ahead, a massive blue clock, its cream face sporting black Roman numerals. The desk, walnut so Solly had boasted, and his green Chesterfield chair on castors, plus the fog of cigar smoke further added to the ambience of a gangster's underground lair where secret business was conducted.

Solly himself, Dracula vibes turned up to the max, had his black hair gelled back with comb stripes, his face pasty-pale. He seemed comfortable with who he was in a mid-blue suit, the pinstripes an inch or so apart, his white grandad-collar shirt leaving no room for a tie. He appeared Italian, or he was trying to give that impression, and the way he sat, one elbow on the arm of his chair, fingertips to his chin, had Ichabod expecting him to say something ominous. Like announcing he had a horse's head ready to put on someone's pillow.

Full coffee cups had been placed in front of them. Ichabod picked his up and took a sip. It tasted bitter. Give him instant Nescafé any day.

Solly sniffed. "So, what the fucking fuck did these Doyle fuckers think they were fucking doing, then?" Pure London accent, no strains of Venice anywhere. He stared at Ichabod. "I've heard a version from your lovely employers here, two of my best fucking friends, I have to say, although we don't get together as much as we should."

The barrage of fuck words beat even George's vocabulary repertoire. Ichabod glanced at George. It seemed it was news to him that Solly was their mate.

Solly pinched his chin, the cleft resembling an arse crack. "So I want to hear it from you now. But first, let me pass on my thanks for the recent information about the Directorates. We'll get to what happened there in a bit. Tell me everything, you Irish tosser." He smiled. "When I call you a tosser, it means I like you."

Ichabod didn't know whether to laugh or not at this bizarre and scary man. "Err…"

He launched into his tale, which took half an hour to spill, Solly studying him all the while, never interrupting except to mutter a fuck or ten.

"So what you're telling me, wanker—and I call people I like a wanker an' all—is that you were threatened—fucking threatened*—into killing a family."* Solly shook his head. *"I mean, fair play to them, they know how to manipulate someone, but I'm offended they chose you. I mean, you're a fucking Cardigan, what they did is below the belt."*

"But they don't know that," George said.

"But we *do,"* Solly huffed, *"and that's enough for me."*

Ichabod didn't understand the fella's logic but sensed he shouldn't question it. How the hell could the Doyles know to not approach him when they weren't aware of who he worked for?

"They just see me as the little eejit they used tae bully when we were kids. They wouldn't think I had the balls tae work for an Estate leader or that I'd even be chosen tae do the job."

"And that's their downfall, prick-face."

Ichabod supposed that name meant Solly liked him, too. He dreaded to think what he called people he despised. Thoughts of the drug swap going down in the early hours of this morning prompted him to say, *"They can't find out I grassed. I can't risk my family bein' hurt."*

"It's all sorted, you cunt. Now let me tell you my *story."* Solly paused at a knock on the door. *"That'll be Bonce with fresh drinks. Come in, you slag!"*

Jaysus…

Bonce, the man who'd shown Ichabod and the twins downstairs, opened the door and walked in bearing a tray. On top, four flutes and a bottle of champagne. How had he known to bring it? Did the room have a camera that linked to upstairs? Had Bonce been watching the proceedings and knew when to appear?

"A bit of a celebration," Solly said.

Bonce popped the cork and poured the drinks, then left in an unsettling, almost glide-like manner. The Italian-not-an-Italian and his slinky butler were doing a number on Ichabod. Screwing with his mind.

"Cheers, ballbags." Solly raised his glass.

Everyone clinked, Ichabod out of his depth; he wanted to go home. George and Greg just sat there as if this was normal. They must be used to Solly from leader meetings.

"Right." Solly gulped the contents of his glass and poured another. *"Tasty fucking stuff, that. So, this is what's gone down on our end. The Directorates were* my *gang, they worked for* me*, except after my best friends here told me what had gone on in Ireland, I had my men poke into them more closely, got one of them*

to open his flapping gums and give a bit of information. The man in question thought my spy wanted an in—stupid dick. They've been selling drugs in Caldraich without my say-so, cutting the product to make it go further, selling powdered-down crap to people in London and the pure shit to those Irish arseholes—no offence to the Irish, but you get what I mean."

Ichabod nodded.

"Patrick wasn't caught by the police today in Folly Courtyard." Solly seemed to expect some encouragement.

"So what happened?" Greg asked.

Solly smiled, clearly pleased someone had played ball. "I had the lot of them Doyle bastards killed, including the father."

Ichabod almost choked on his champagne. "Um, my cousin never said."

"What, Rowan?"

Jaysus, how did Solly know his name?

Solly grinned. "I do my due diligence, you tosspot. I look into everyone I'm dealing with before I make a move, like any proper leader should. And Rowan won't have told you because I doubt he'll know they're dead yet. This mess went only went down at four a.m."

George chuckled. "Have you done it so they've gone 'missing'?"

"No. They'll be found. Eventually. When someone bothers to notice they're not around."

"They will," Ichabod said. "They're regulars in the pub."

"Where are they?" Greg asked.

"My men stuffed them in the Doyles' fucking loft, didn't they. Wedged them between all manner of shit up there. One of them is in a pile beside an old rocking horse. I've got pictures. Anyway, they were hacked to death while the drop at the Folly was taking place, all of them disoriented because they were woken up and hauled out of bed. Two of my other men met with Patrick — what an utter ponce he is, by the way. Tried to make out, when my blokes dragged him down an alley, that he wasn't anything to do with it. Claimed innocence, yet he'd turned up at fucking-fuck o'clock with no explanation. Sod that noise." Solly displayed his veneers. Necked his champagne. "My booze not good enough for you?" He nodded to the other three glasses which were still mostly full.

"Your story's so riveting, we forgot to drink," George said.

Ichabod picked up on the sarcasm, but it seemed Solly hadn't.

The oddball grinned, clearly pleased he'd spun a good yarn. "I was going to say, that's a bottle of fucking Bolly and isn't to be sniffed at. So, where was I? Oh, yeah. Old Patrick, he was carted off to a van and taken to the hills. I expect the early birds have had a good peck at him by now—he was chopped up, too—but no doubt one of them rambling weirdo types will find him soon. My men were in and out of Ireland pretty sharpish, back in the UK for brunch."

Ichabod took a steadying breath. The Doyles and Patrick, dead? He hadn't expected this at all. "Aoife, Patrick's wife, she'll probably think he's gone off somewhere again, like he had tae last week when he took the drugs tae Limerick."

Solly nodded. "All's good, then. She might not report him missing for a while."

Annoyed, because it meant the Doyles had got away with it again—all right, they were dead and couldn't hurt anyone else, but it still meant they wouldn't be caught for their crimes by Shay and the garda—Icabod had to force himself to be happy about what Solly had arranged. Caldraich was going to erupt with gossip soon when the Doyles and Patrick didn't show up.

"As for the Limerick lot. They'll get what's coming to them." Solly frowned. "So, do I get a thanks?"

"Thanks," Ichabod said, almost saying 'go raibh maith agat' instead because he hadn't quite shifted back into his London world. Caldraich was still very much on his mind and would be for a while to come.

"Glad you said that." Solly sighed. "Ungrateful people do my nut in." He paused. Studied Ichabod again. "You're a good sort, bollock-knob. Pleasure to have helped you, because, let's face it, you helped me find out I had a shitload of traitors in my circle, so I repaid the favour."

"What's happened to them? The Directorates?" Ichabod asked.

"Dead, the lot of them, and this time, no one will find them. Shot them all in the bastard knees, then their faces. I've got to choose others now to take their place. They'll be told their fate before they start work so if they ever think of fucking me about, they know the score from the fucking off. Now then." He smiled at George then Greg. "How about we get together for a good old knees-up?"

"Yeah." George drank his champagne and stood. "We'll be in touch."

Greg finished his drink, as did Ichabod, and Bonce appeared like an earwigging stalker and escorted them upstairs.

In the back seat of the BMW, Ichabod let out a sigh of relief. "He's a strange feckin' fella."

"Yep, he's a dickhead. Thinks he's Vito Corleone." George revved the engine. "Still, he got the job done, and now everyone's safe from the Doyles."

No one spoke on the journey to Cardigan. Ichabod pondered on whether to tell Shay about this, about where the bodies were, but decided against it. Shay was garda, and a Clancy, and no matter that Solly had done Caldraich a solid because of Ichabod's tip-off, Shay would probe him as to how he knew about those bodies.

It was too much of a risk to open his mouth.

Dropped off at his place, he went inside and stared at his poky living quarters. Maybe, now he'd shown the twins he was loyal by contacting them about the Directorates, they might see him in a different light. A shiner one. And offer him a tug up the rung of the Cardigan ladder.

Chapter Twenty-Three

The connecting door to the garage opened. Ichabod held his breath and stared through the tiny gap between the kitchen door and the fridge-freezer. There was no way he'd be seen, but he *felt* seen, even though the little space was cloaked in darkness. Marleigh entered first, her face showing signs of strain, upset, and fatigue. She placed her handbag on the island and flicked her gaze around, trying to find him. Ichabod released his breath slowly. If she gave it away at the last minute…

David came in. Sharp suit. Bit of a tan. Brazil must be hot in December. Apart from the obvious tension in his face, he looked well-rested, as if being with the other woman was a tonic. Ichabod understood how that worked. When he was with Marleigh, he felt different. Did David's mistress provide the same for him?

The urge to burst out of his hiding place and launch himself at the man gripped Ichabod. But he stayed put. David shut the connecting door. Didn't lock it. Why? Was he planning a swift exit? Where would he even go if he ripped Marleigh's heart in two and left her here to cry alone? Yes, she was used to being by herself, but to abandon her, knowing she might be devastated… Bastard behaviour.

"We'll talk in the living room," Marleigh said.

Proud she was taking control and not giving it to her husband, Ichabod smiled.

David scowled. "I'm warning you, there's a lot to say."

"I'm sure there is."

"More than you'd like."

"Mm-hmm."

David shook his head as though he hated her, hated her calm demeanour. Was that because she was forcing him to explain himself? Because she wasn't being good little Marleigh, acting whatever way he wanted? The way he was used to? Or had he fallen for the other woman, and now Marleigh was surplus to requirements he couldn't stand to look at her because guilt strangled him with both hands?

If he even feels guilty.

Still, one man's loss was another man's gain. She was Ichabod's now.

Man and wife went out of view.

Ichabod left his cubby hole and moved to the doorway. He paused to listen.

"So tell me," Marleigh said. "All of it."

"What I told you in the car is true. About Mr Weed."

Ichabod hoped the man wasn't going to skip over that bit. He had no idea what had been said in the car and needed to know.

"That as a teenager you worked for someone with a ridiculous name, flying all over the place to collect drugs, and you stopped doing it when you met me. Why?"

"Because I'd just landed my day job, didn't need the money."

"Oh, so it wasn't because you didn't want to get me in the shit along with you? You didn't want to protect me from the fact you're a scummy drug trafficker? Charming."

"I could have carried on, but I wanted to spend all my spare time with you. We were good then, you can't deny it."

Ichabod didn't want to think of a time those two had been good together.

"Yes, it was perfect," she said. "It didn't hurt that I was a kept woman either. But there's something I have to tell you about that. I want to preface it by saying I did love you—"

"Did?"

"Let me finish. I did love you, but I chose you because of your money. That first date, you told me how much you earned—maybe you were bragging, or maybe you were just that excited about it—but it put my fears to rest. I'd never go without, I'd be safe, never have to worry about bills."

"So you *used* me?"

"In a way, but I ended up falling in love with you."

"Thanks for that." David sounded sarcastic. "That's brilliant, knowing you were a gold-digger and I didn't pick up on it."

"Like I didn't pick up on your shady past? We're even there. No need to beat ourselves up about our shortcomings when we were younger."

"All these years I could have—"

"Could have what? Been with someone else like you are now?"

"Pardon?"

"You heard me. Perfume gives the game away. You might want to remember that for future reference when you cheat on *her*, too."

"I've never smelled of perfume unless it's yours."

"You might *think* that, but you did. You do now. I can show you the exact day I smelled it if you like."

"What?"

"I've kept a diary all this time, right from when we first met."

"What else is in it?"

"The dates you went away, when you got back. Quite a little gem for the police, wouldn't you say?"

"Give it to me."

"No."

"Are you going to the police?"

"No."

"Why, because of the *shame*?"

Ichabod tensed. David was taking the piss out of her, drawing out one of her flaws to belittle her. Okay, the fella was likely hurt because of her confession about using him, but he had more wrongs on his rap sheet than she did. She *had* loved him, it hadn't all been a money-grab situation. Going with a man for life security, while devious, wasn't as bad as drugs and another family, was it?

"Why are you being so cruel?" Marleigh asked quietly. "As if I'm the one on trial here. I've admitted what *I* did."

"So have I."

"No, there's still the issue of the perfume."

A sigh. "I'd planned to tell you this today anyway, so fuck it."

"Tell me what? That you've been having an affair? That you've probably got a brood of kids?"

"Just the one."

Silence. The air thrummed with tension, or maybe that thrum was Ichabod's anger pushing blood through his system, fast, buzzing in his ears. It rankled that he wasn't in the room with her to soften the blow with his hand holding hers.

Sobs. Great wrenching sobs. Oh God, she'd broken down. Did that mean she still cared? Had she secretly harboured wanting kids, and finding out David had one sliced a wound in her? David had succeeded in breaking her strong façade. Did he feel good about that? Putting her in her place once and for all? Getting her back for her confession with one of his own?

"How old?" she asked, her voice cracking.

"Six months. A boy."

"Oh, so that was what that grin was in aid of."

"What?"

"One night, six months ago, you got a phone call. I suppose that was when your son was born. And the mother? Who is she?"

"A Brazilian. I've been seeing her for three years."

"When you changed."

"Yes."

"I knew it. I wasn't going mad after all."

"I'd say I'm sorry, but I'm actually not. She's—"

"I don't need to know what or who she is." Another sigh. Juddery. "I'll keep this house, thank you."

"I was going to sign it over to you anyway."

"How magnanimous of you."

"Considering you've admitted you're a gold-digger, I should change my mind, but I won't."

"Why, to pay me off? Pay for my silence? To make me go away so you can trip off into the sunset, guilt-free?"

"Something like that. I've already got an apartment in Wapping."

"Of course you have. You were never one to leave things to chance. Always one step ahead." A pause. "Let me ask you. About that refugee we saw at the window in Golden Glow. Was it because she was foreign that you wanted to help her? Did she remind you of your new woman?"

Ichabod recalled how the refugee had written *pomoc* (help) in Polish in the condensation from her breath on the glass.

"Maybe that was a subconscious act," David said.

Marleigh laughed. "Even then I believed you still loved me. We'd been talking about a deal with your job, do you remember?"

Why is she reminiscing? Is she tryin' tae get him tae think of the good times?

"Yep."

"But all the while you'd been *shagging someone else*. You disgust me."

Relieved she hadn't tried to get David back onside, Ichabod relaxed a tad. Movement to his right smudged his peripheral vision. He turned, recognising two big shapes through the patterned glass in the front door. He walked slowly, letting the twins in. Pointed towards the living room. George and Greg, in their beards and wigs, crept down the hallway.

Ichabod followed.

The Brothers burst into the room.

David, standing by the window looking out, spun round in shock. "Who the devil are *you*?"

"You got the devil bit right," George said. "I'm George Wilkes, and this is my brother, Greg." He turned to look at Ichabod, winking. "And this man here is your executioner."

Chapter Twenty-Four

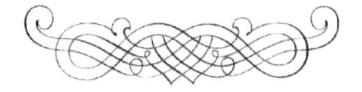

David, his wrists and ankles cable-tied, lay in the boot of his car where those two brick shithouse men had thrown him. Why did they have beards and wigs on? Was it so the neighbours couldn't identify them? Had they paid them a visit, offering money so they stayed silent? Because someone would have clocked them arriving. What had Marleigh done, phoned them once she'd read what was in the ledger? For the first time he cursed them being a good couple, reporting that poor refugee woman's plea for help to the police. If Marleigh hadn't had the twins' number, he doubted this would be happening. Although she could have called the police instead, and she would have done. She hated drugs.

The way he'd been placed in here, his back to the opening of the boot, meant he couldn't use his feet to kick out at the brake lights, nor could he use his hands. One of the men had used wire to secure the cable tie on his wrist to the buttonhole of his shirt, binding his hands to his chest. He'd tried nutting the lid in an attempt to get someone to hear the thudding, but he doubted it would carry, given the speed he judged they were going.

Marleigh hadn't appeared shocked then the twins had come into the living room. More like smug, her smile dark and mysterious, switching to triumphant when it was clear David had realised this was the end of the drug road for him—for good, because after they'd beaten him up or whatever it was they planned to do, they'd be watching him. Maybe even incarcerate him somewhere as a lesson. What had one of them said? They'd take him to a warehouse?

At least with the police he'd have gone to prison and could have written to Janaína, explaining where he was and what had happened, but this way, she wouldn't find out until The Brothers released him. The Wapping flat was in his name, not hers, and he hadn't even told her the address, so if she came to the UK to find him—or her scary-as-fuck brothers did— she'd have to stay in a hotel, unless Mr Weed put her up. Then there was the rent on the house in Brazil that he paid for, the Posh Pad as he called it. The money wouldn't go into her account because he'd bet his phone would be taken away from him, preventing his usual transfer on the app, and she'd immediately become suspicious.

Her brothers, two men who worked for the drug outfit over there, had warned him not to mess with her. They'd told him to leave his wife and make an honest woman out of their sister once their nephew had been born. Yes, they'd come looking, maybe even visit the house and ask Marleigh questions. What would she say? The truth?

No, she'd keep it to herself. That conversation she'd had with the Irishman had stuck with David.

"Ye stay here, because when the body is found, ye need tae have an alibi."

"But if no one's here with me, how can I prove I was home?"

"Go out and put rubbish in ye wheelie bin, or wash ye car so someone sees ye. Do a bit of weedin' in the front garden."

"Okay."

David jolted at the memory, something he hadn't registered at the time because he'd been too interested in watching how Marleigh and the man were interacting, as if there was something between them. The thought of her having an affair with him while David had been away had incensed him. Now, though…

When the body is found…

Shit. That Irishman really was going to kill him.

Chapter Twenty-Five

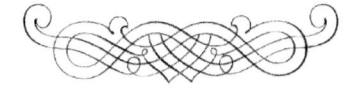

George had said he'd leave the torture *and* killing to Ichabod. That was new, allowing him to torture by himself. Ichabod reckoned it was a test, to see how far he was prepared to go. Did that mean George had other plans for him? Letting Rowan take over running Jackpot Palace because Ichabod would be better use elsewhere?

Am I prepared tae do it?

Yes.

David stood where the wooden chair was usually placed. He was clothed, but George instructed him to remove each item and pass it his way so they could be placed in a plastic bag large enough to hold it all.

"Transference," George said to Ichabod while David begrudgingly disrobed, Greg holding a gun pointed at him to ensure he didn't get any funny ideas. "Got to make sure nothing from this place gets on his clobber. I'm trying to be more forensically aware when we're delivering bodies. Bloody interesting stuff. Have you ever looked it up?"

"No."

"Maybe you should. For the future."

Ichabod nodded.

David passed George his clothing one by one. He stood, naked, his hands covering his meat and two veg. George put the bag on the end of the tool table and returned with the wooden chair.

Ichabod didn't waste any time. He launched a roundhouse kick at David, following it up with other moves in his ninja bag of tricks. By the time he'd finished, David had split lips, bruising, and a squidgy lump on his temple.

"All right!" David said. "I get it!"

"I don't think you do." George forced him onto the chair, strapped him to the back with rope, then he went off to set up what Ichabod had requested, chuckling every so often. "I wish I'd thought of this. I might well do it myself one day."

David's cock and balls shrivelled through fear and undoubtedly the cold as it had just got pretty chilly in here. He shivered, but that was understandable. Ichabod had asked for a standing fan, with a hessian bag of ice hanging on the front, to be placed behind the cheating bastard. The freezing air whacked into David's back, ruffling the hair at the sides of his head.

Why had Ichabod asked for that? He'd been thinking since George had spoken to him when Katy had been here, and he'd come up with the cold air…just because. It would appeal to George's sense of humour plus prove Ichabod was willing to do nonsensical things for shits and giggles. Anyway, he liked seeing David suffer, his teeth chattering, goosebumps all over the visible skin, his lips with a blue tinge around the edges.

It was weird being in a forensic suit, although it did give Ichabod the deluded sense that he was on the right side of the law here—he could pretend he was doing this legally, and maybe that was how he should view it going forward. Distancing himself further from the Sullivan crime where he'd had his own clothes on.

A different kettle of fish altogether.

He cocked his head to study David who wouldn't meet his eye. A coward, then, this up-his-own-arse prick who'd hurt Marleigh so badly. George moved round the front, standing back a bit. He snorted laughter, which gave Ichabod the fuel he needed to continue.

"What were ye thinkin', treatin' ye precious wife like that?"

"I...I d-didn't e-expect her to f-f-find out."

Ichabod smothered a smile at the fella not being able to talk properly due to the temperature. "What, about the drugs or the other woman?"

"The d-drugs. I w-was always g-going to t-tell her about J-J-Janaína."

"When it suited ye. And does this Janaína know ye're married?"

"Y-yes."

"And it doesn't bother her?"

"N-no. S-she knows the m-marriage was over when I m-met her."

Ichabod glanced at George for clarification on that.

George smiled. "Mason told us Janaína has been squealing nicely after he informed her you weren't going to leave Marleigh after all."

"W-what? No! That's a lie!"

"I know, shit breath," George said. "Some women get the hump when told that sort of thing, which is why I ordered for it to be said. Anyway, she let rip and gave us some valuable information. That you've been seeing her ever since you started up with Mr Weed again. Three years. She said you made it obvious you fancied her well before that, but she was in a relationship, so neither of you did anything about the attraction."

Ichabod took over. "So ye were prepared tae be unfaithful to Marleigh at a time when she thought ye were still in love? Years before she even knew there was a problem? Ye said the marriage was over when ye started fancyin' Janaína, yet it was before that. If ye didn't love

Marleigh at that point, why stay wid her? Ye're a feckin' bastard."

"It doesn't c-count if you j-just fancy s-someone."

Ichabod smiled. "So it doesn't count if Marleigh fancied *me* when she worked with us on the Goldie job?"

David scowled. "That's different."

"Why?"

"Because it j-just is."

"I see. Grand for you but not for her. Right." Ichabod sneered. "Eejit."

He held his hand out for the craft knife George held. Thought about carving FUCKBAG in David's brow, proving to George he could be the same as him. Just as mean. Just as deadly.

"Can ye hold his head steady for me?"

George complied, standing behind David and clamping him tight. Ichabod straddled David's legs and speared the tip of the knife into a patch of skin on the forehead, waiting for the man to moan.

"Oh God… Oh God…"

The sound of trickling fluid and the stench of piss didn't need any explanation. The man was terrified.

"Filthy cunt," George muttered.

Ichabod drew the F, and as David got used to the pain, he wrote the other letters.

George peered down. "Fuckbag?" He roared with laughter, digging his gloved fingertip into the lines, tracing them, until he'd reached the end of the G. "I bet that's sore."

"Who's Mr Weed?" Ichabod asked.

"Please, I don't know, that's the name he told me to call him."

The stuttering had stopped, so maybe David was nice and heated from the flush that would have swept through him from the pain. Sweat coated his cheeks.

"Has he always worn a balaclava?"

"Yes, I swear."

"How did ye get involved wid him?"

"He put an advert in the paper, wanting teens to do paper rounds."

"And when ye got there it was…what?"

"Selling drugs at first, then he sent me abroad."

"Where did ye meet up wid him?"

"In a lock-up."

"The one ye drove tae earlier?"

"Yes."

Ichabod looked at George who still held David's head, pressing his meaty, gloved fingers into the nasty bulge at the temple. David yelped.

"He's been workin' from there for a long time." Ichabod tutted. "Feckin' hell." He knew who the man was now, the name whispered to him as the twins had bundled David into the boot of his car at Marleigh's. "All done behind ye back."

"Don't worry about it," George said. "We're dealing with him later. Or at least figuring out what to do."

"Who is he?" David asked, clearly playing for time.

"None of ye feckin' business. Where do the drugs get sold?"

"The Cardigan Estate. He didn't want the gear on his patch."

George stared at the ceiling, a muscle in his jaw flexing. "You know, some people are such cheeky twunts, taking liberties."

Ichabod attacked David's cheeks, slicing them more than George had done to Katy's, to prove a point, that he could go one step further, he was willing and able, even if a small part of him cringed at what he was doing. Anger overtook him on Marleigh's behalf, and he slashed and slashed, hitting jawbone and teeth, the blade shooting across to sever the septum. His head filled with a buzzing noise, drowning out any screams David released. All that mattered was wrecking this bastard's face.

The ire faded quickly, though, and Ichabod stepped away, the flush of adrenaline disappearing and sending his legs weak. David whimpered and wailed, but Ichabod had no sympathy for him. The man deserved everything he got.

George took a picture of him, a close-up of the savaged flesh. He shouted over the noise, "Janaína asked for proof we'd fucked you up. Maybe she'll throw darts at it for fun."

David hung his head, blood dripping onto the rope around his torso, on his dick, his bollocks, his thighs. Another stream of piss erupted, diluting the claret. It trickled onto the floor, pink, splashing, stinking with the sharp tang of desperation and outright fear. Ichabod gripped the end of the penis and pulled to elongate it.

"This is for Marleigh," he yelled to be heard over David's racket. A quick slice, and the cock came away, blood surging from the remaining wound and dribbling from the penis. He glanced at George, nodding.

George tipped David's head back.

Ichabod had promised himself he's slit this fecker's throat.

And with one swipe of the blade, he did just that.

Chapter Twenty-Six

At an emergency meeting later that afternoon, George and Greg had invited all of the Estate leaders bar Solly Moss—Mr Weed, SUV number plate 5 MO55. They sat around the tool table, cans of Coke in front of everyone. This was going to be short and sweet. When one leader went against the others, it wasn't unusual for that person to be shot by every other leader, the body disposed of. Solly's lot had been dealing on Cardigan without permission, so he was royally fucked.

"Sorry to be so vague in the message," George said, "but once you've heard what I've got to say, you'll understand my need for you to keep this meeting to yourself and not tell Solly. Because of Moon's absence—he's still in Amsterdam—Greg will be taking the minutes so he knows what's going on. All agreed?"

A flurry of yesses followed.

"Right, Solly Moss has a drug gang called the Directorates, we all know that. He assured us the drugs don't get flogged anywhere in London apart from his own Estate. He lied. He's been selling on Cardigan for years."

"Fucking wanker," someone muttered.

"That's one word for him." George smiled then went on to fill them in on everything, including the Ireland bollocks. "We've just apprehended one of his traffickers. He touched down from Brazil this morning. We've got a ledger he kept of all the times he went abroad and how much he brought in. What it was—coke. The trafficker is dead—one of my men had a bit of fun there. Who's in line to take over The Moss Estate?"

Evan Cardinal raised a hand. "Where's the trafficker going to end up?"

"He'll be found by whoever in Daffodil Woods. Dog walker. Jogger. The reason we didn't chuck him in the Thames is because his wife, who is innocent in all this and grassed him up to us, will need to claim the life insurance. We don't want her going without, waiting seven years for him to be pronounced legally dead. She did the right thing by telling us so should be rewarded. As for Solly, he'll disappear as usual after we've all taken a shot at him. Everyone in agreement?"

At their nods and ayes, George continued. "We all know he'll try to talk his way out of it, but I have so much proof that I don't feel we need to interrogate him. I suggest we shoot him as soon as he sits down at this table."

"How are we going to get him here?" Cardinal again.

"Last time we saw him outside of a leader meeting, he mentioned us being his best friends—news to me and Greg—and that we needed to go out for a drink. I'll give him a bell and organise that. It was a fair while ago, and he'll probably point that out, but who gives a fuck about his hurt feelings? We could meet at the

Noodle and Tiger—no cameras in that area at all, which is one of the reasons why we bought the place—and we'll drive him here in our taxi. You'll all be waiting."

"When?"

"Is tonight too soon? I want shot of him ASAP. Pardon the pun."

No one uttered an objection.

George grinned. "Sorted. Be here for eight o'clock. With guns."

Chapter Twenty-Seven

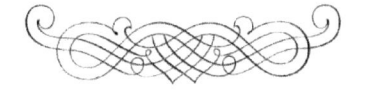

Janine stood beside the body of a naked man at the crime scene, knowing who he was, what he'd done, and who'd killed him. Who'd fucked him right up. Lately, that had been the story of her life. She understood why yet another of the twins' corpses had been left for someone to find, as Marleigh needed the life insurance payout, but things had just got worrying.

"Another note," Jim, the pathologist, said. He stared at it. Someone had held it down by placing a stone at one corner. "In a sandwich bag like the others."

Janine stared at it, too, the words visible through the transparent plastic.

VICTIM JUST GOT HOME FROM A LITTLE DRUG TRIP TO BRAZIL.

This...*this* Janine didn't need, all the shit that would come with the note being present. Why hadn't the twins just dumped David so the case presented as a regular murder they could blame on this Mr Weed eventually? Why had they gone against her wishes and relied on the note method, linking this kill to several in the past? It had already become obvious that there was a vigilante out there, a narrative she'd planted in the minds of her colleagues, but she couldn't be doing with her DCI finally telling her she needed to find out who it was, open an active file on it rather than it being on a to-do list. It would be an investigation of deliberate dead ends, ones she created, a headache she didn't want.

Yes, it was definitely time to step back from being the twins' copper. She was suddenly so *tired* of doing this. Living on her nerves. Watching every step she took. It wasn't fun anymore. Didn't give her the satisfaction it used to. If they refused to play ball when she was the one having to deal with the fallout, then they didn't 'like' her as much as they'd claimed. If they did, they'd prefer to keep her onside.

But George always wanted things his own way. Like her, he needed to be in control, and she understood that more than the average person, but this was the last time she was struggling through a murder case, knowing the ins and outs of it yet pretending to her team, Jim, and the SOCO scene manager, Sheila Sutton, that she was as clueless as them.

Bryan Flint had better take up their offer.

"He wasn't killed here." Jim glanced over at SOCOs who wrestled a tent from the van. "Barely any blood, and going by the slashes on his face and the one across his throat, there would have been a lot. Whoever did it had a beef. It says Fuckbag on his forehead."

Janine's lips twitched.

"The vigilante again." Sheila sighed.

"Yes. The note points to whoever is doing this. Same writing," Jim said.

Ichabod had written all of the past ones, and she imagined he'd had great pleasure writing this one, too. Killing David would have been satisfying for him. Marleigh could finally be his now, if the woman even wanted him. Janine wasn't in the know about the state of play there, she was only aware that Ichabod had a thing for her. Was it because she was so pretty? An older woman? What had drawn him to her?

Janine puffed air out, her mask inflating. "While this person is doing us a favour with the information in the notes, telling us what the victim has done, it begs the question how they know about these people in the first place. Doesn't the vigilante have a job? How has he got the time to gather the information needed before he kills?"

Colin shuffled beside her. "So you're saying it's a man."

"It's the most likely scenario," Sheila said. "Women killers are rare."

"But not unheard of," Colin retorted.

Janine would grab this chance to run with that, get any suspicion off the twins. Jim had once put their names forward as the perpetrators, and it was the main reason why she'd urged them to pack this shit in. All right, at times she'd needed bodies because they'd tied in with cases she'd worked on, but David wasn't on anyone's radar as far as she knew. Mind you, the National Drugs Intelligence Unit might have been looking into him for however long. She'd soon find out. Now his body lay here, she had an excuse to speak to the NDIU officer on that case, if there was one.

It would piss her off something chronic if she found out David would have been apprehended by the drug squad soon. His death wouldn't have had to happen. She wouldn't be in this position now.

Of course you would be. George wouldn't want to let David go to prison.

"Fair point, Col," she said. "Yes, women killers *are* rare, but you could be onto something there."

Sheila scoffed. "She'd have to be pretty strong to do half of what's gone on, here and in the past. I mean, his bruises. He's had the shit beaten out of him. And can a woman—no disrespect intended—have the strength to hang someone?"

"But he hasn't been hanged," Jim said.

"I'm thinking about Peter Ford's death recently."

"He killed himself," Jim reminded her.

"It was just an example," Sheila bristled, "to prove my theory that based on all those bodies left by the vigilante, it *has* to be a man."

Peter's death had been set up to look like a suicide. The postmortem report had matched that scenario because George had hung Peter in the warehouse so the marks on the neck matched those he would have got in the location where they'd left him. Janine had been so relieved about that as Jim was excellent at his job and usually spotted inconsistencies. It had been down to George's genius and forethought that the outcome had been what she'd needed. The suicide note, written by Peter under duress, may have subconsciously swayed Jim into going down that route.

"I'm going to keep a woman in mind anyway," Janine said. "Cover all bases until we know otherwise."

Sheila snorted. "This person is forensically aware. Not once has my team found anything that could be linked to the killer."

Bloody good job an' all.

"Yet another penis has been cut off, though." Colin crossed his arms. "That speaks of a woman to me. What's the bet this geezer's had an affair."

Janine stared at the limp sausage of flesh in David's mouth.

Sheila all but growled. "But— Oh, sod it. I can see I'm wasting my breath."

"Are you okay?" Janine asked her. "You don't seem yourself today."

"It's Noah. He's been poorly, and Becky's not been getting much sleep. Neither have I because she phoned me about it during the night."

Becky was Sheila's niece, Noah her great-nephew.

"Sorry to hear that."

Sheila waved it away.

Janine gestured to David's clothes, left in a folded stack beside him. "Another vigilante thing, that neat pile. Would a man necessarily do that? Fold them? All the blokes I know would just drop them in a heap."

Colin chuckled. "Yep, I would. The missus is always banging on at me about that."

"I don't blame her," Janine said. "She isn't a maid. She shouldn't have to pick up after you."

"I knew you'd take her side," he grumped.

Janine switched subjects. "Anyway, can you have a nose for ID, please, Jim?"

Jim changed his gloves, as did Sheila. Between them, they looked through each piece of clothing and, finding nothing so far, Sheila bagged the items. Suit trousers, the last thing to be checked, provided what Janine needed. A wallet.

Jim opened it and pulled out a credit card. "A Mr David Jasper."

"Oh," Janine blurted for effect. "That surname rings a bell. I'm sure it's the same one in the refugee case where a woman rang in about that poor cow in Golden Glow."

"Jesus, he could be a Minion for The Network," Colin said. "That'd mean there's only two of them left to find."

Janine nodded. "We'll go and see his wife now. Marleigh, if memory serves."

"I hate those visits." Colin grunted. "Telling people someone's died. Most DIs leave it to uniforms, but not you."

"I prefer doing it, you know that," Janine snapped. "Besides, we have to speak to her about David. Find out if she ever suspected him of being in The Network. We can seize his laptop or whatever, see if there's anything on it. The note mentions drugs. Maybe the information we need will be on there about that, too."

She said her goodbyes and left the tent, already planning what she'd say to the twins about them leaving that note. What the *fuck* were they thinking?

Or specifically, George. Was that move a little dig at her for announcing they'd have to find another copper? Was that the only reason he'd done it, to piss her off?

Hmm, highly probable. He was childish like that.

Janine sat in Marleigh's living room on a sofa, Colin beside her. Marleigh and her mother, Fern, occupied the other couch. Both women had similar features, although Marleigh was blonde, Fern going grey.

The news of David's murder had been delivered to Marleigh before Fern had arrived, plus the explanation of how he'd died. Bruising on his body, as if he'd been in a fight, his face stabbed, a sliced neck, and his penis cut off. Marleigh had played a blinder in front of Colin, crumpling at the description, sobbing into her hands. At that point Janine had suggested someone come and sit with her while they talked, hence the mother being here. She lived a couple of streets away and had driven round immediately. Marleigh had given Fern a garbled account of what had happened. Fern had appeared shocked and confused.

"Do you know of anyone who'd do that to him?" Janine asked.

Marleigh nodded. "I think…I think he was doing something with drugs."

"*Drugs?*" Fern belted out. "*David?*"

Marleigh stared at her. "It was as much a shock to me as it is for you, Mum."

"How long have you known?" Fern asked.

"I found a ledger in his safe. I was waiting to confront him about it."

"Waiting?" Fern asked. "Why?"

"Because I lied. We didn't spend Christmas alone together. He buggered off abroad, and I was left here on my own."

"Oh, darling, why didn't you say?"

Marleigh gave a slight roll of her eyes. "Because it was embarrassing. I didn't want anyone to know. Anyway, I *did* confront him, but he stormed out. The ledger mentions cocaine and heroin."

"That's helpful," Janine said. "I'll need to take that."

Fern stood. "I'll get it. Where is it?"

Marleigh looked up at her. "On my bedside table."

Janine took a pair of gloves from her pocket. "Put these on, please."

Fern appeared aggrieved but slipped them on and left.

Janine nudged Colin to get his notebook out. "Tell me what happened today, Marleigh."

"I went to the airport; I couldn't wait until he got home. Once I knew what he'd been up to, I wanted to talk about it as soon as possible. I found his car and waited in it."

"How did you get there?"

"I took a black cab."

Janine almost sagged in relief. The twins would have worked it so their taxi was caught on camera, fake plates, bolstering Marleigh's account of events. She only hoped it would be sighted showing Marleigh getting out of it, but if it didn't, Janine would have to work around it. Fudge a few things. *I have to make sure her movements today are provable.* But what if they hadn't taken her? Ichabod could have driven her. *Shit.* "Go on."

"He only took a small suitcase away with him, yet he had a bigger one with him, too. He seemed shocked to see me, obviously, because I never go to meet him. He put the cases in the boot and got in the driver's side." Marleigh went on to explain her version—the one George and Greg would have coached her on, or maybe they'd used Ichabod for that.

"So he admitted to bringing drugs in from Brazil?" Janine checked.

"Yes, and to seeing another woman who he has a baby with. She lives in Brazil from what I could gather. I told him to get out, and like I said, he stormed off. He went in the car."

"Did he give you any clue as to who he worked for?"

"Someone called Mr Weed."

Colin chuckled, and Janine kicked his foot.

"Right, obviously an alias." *And someone David's murder will be pinned on.* Janine was about to speak again but stopped herself as Fern reappeared.

The woman handed her the ledger. "I had a look inside. I didn't believe he was capable of this until I read it. I had to see for myself."

"Good job you had gloves on, then," Janine said wryly. "If you hadn't, it may have indicated you were implicated, what with your fingerprints being on it."

"I would *never*!"

Satisfied she'd made her point, Janine addressed Marleigh. "Do you know where David might have gone after he left here?"

"He said he had a flat in Wapping, which was news to me. Probably for him and his secret little family."

Fern sat and rested an arm around her daughter's shoulders. "Honestly, this is all such a shock. A woman and a son abroad. I thought he had to fly out regularly for work."

"He did," Marleigh said. "Just not as often." She glanced at Janine. "You can ask his boss, Harry — his proper boss, not that Mr Weed — and he'll be able to give you the times and dates of the legitimate trips. I went on some of those with him. Usually to Vegas." She scrunched her eyes closed. "We had *such* a good time there, some of my best memories, and now they're tainted."

"So you came straight home from the airport," Janine stated.

"No, he said he had to drop something off for Harry. He drove to a row of lock-ups behind some houses in Canning Town. An SUV was there, black, and two men got out of it. They had balaclavas on, which frightened me. They went into the middle lock-up. David took the larger suitcase in with him."

"Can you remember exactly where that was?"

"Sorry, no. My head was all over the place because we'd had a row in the car, plus those balaclavas scared me."

While the team investigated the possible route, it would give Janine time to consult the twins to find out whether there was a likelihood their taxi, van, or BMW had been spotted in the vicinity. Yet another hurdle for her to navigate.

"Why didn't you leave the car?" Colin asked. "I mean, you saw men in balaclavas. That's enough to make anyone run."

"I don't know." Marleigh bit her bottom lip.

It seemed Colin was actually prepared to do a bit of work today. "Apart from what you've read in the papers about The Network, do you have any reason to think David would have been involved?"

"Oh my God!" Fern shrieked. "This just gets worse!"

Marleigh shook her head. "No."

"Where have you been since your husband 'stormed out'?" Colin asked.

Janine could have brained him. Yes, he was doing his job, but she wished he'd fuck off and be quiet like he usually was.

Marleigh frowned. "I was here."

Colin shifted to the edge of his seat. "Only, we have to consider, seeing as your husband admitted to having an affair, and the fact his penis has been cut off—"

"What my colleague is saying is we would usually suspect the wife in this instance because the penis issue could indicate an angry reaction to being cheated on. So long as your neighbours can corroborate that you didn't leave after David, everything will be fine."

"And if they can't?" Fern asked.

"Then we'll check ANPR for her vehicle, amongst other avenues." Janine smiled. "I don't believe you had anything to do with this, but we have to go through the motions anyway."

They spoke for a while longer, Janine cutting it short when Marleigh broke down again, Janine saying they'd leave her to digest the news in private. In reality, she needed to get out of the house, stop at a café and send Colin off to buy coffees and a bit of food to stuff his face with so she could message George and Greg in private. If she knew what she was supposed to be avoiding, this investigation might be plain sailing.

Outside, armed with David's laptop, she spotted Cameron parked up the road. He smiled, likely still pleased as punch at the baby news. She smiled back, vowing to get this case sorted quickly to reduce her anxiety levels. She had a child to think of now, and if George didn't like it when she told him this was the last time she'd do anything major for them, then tough.

Like Cameron had said, her health was the important thing now, and the baby's. And she'd get over not being the twins' copper eventually.

Here's hoping Flint agrees to take my place and they prefer him over me. Then I won't have to go back to work for them.

She was pleasantly surprised how happy that made her, considering her previous thoughts on the subject. It was time to play happy families. To finally accept that she wasn't damaged goods and could lead the life other people led.

She *was* good enough.

Chapter Twenty-Eight

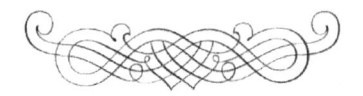

The Feud – Part One

Aoife wandered along Corduroy Road on this life-changing Saturday in the gloominess of a winter morning, her thick coat, scarf, and fur-lined boots keeping out the cold. Although another type of cold had chilled her yesterday evening, one no amount of clothing or heating could shift. She worked in her father's pub, the Fiddler's, and had overheard something she shouldn't. A drunk man telling another his woes.

A man she'd been having an affair with.

The news had devastated her. She'd thought he was going to leave his wife for her, but it seemed he'd been dipping his wick in three women. Wife, Mistress One, and Mistress Two. Were there others? It would be hard to tell as the villagers were so secretive in some respects.

She headed towards the Sullivan farm, on her way to see Caoimhe. She could have got a taxi, but she didn't want her husband to know where she was going. The only taxi driver in the village talked too much, plus Patrick might have seen her getting into the car. As far as he was aware, she'd gone to see a friend a few streets away, a woman he disliked, who he didn't speak to, so he wouldn't query her as to whether Aoife had been there. Nollaig knew about the affair, just not who the man was.

Aoife wouldn't dump *this* secret on her, though. It was too big. Too much.

Caoimhe Sullivan was another matter. They'd been firm friends since they were children, along with Erin Doyle, although for this, for what Aoife had to say, well, only Caoimhe could know. There were some people you trusted with your life, you knew they'd stick with you no matter what, and Caoimhe was one of them. Aoife should know. The woman knew what had been going on for months behind certain backs and had never breathed a word.

Lorcan, along with little Finn and Darragh, had gone to the next town over, Caoimhe sending them off on a day out. Swimming then a visit to the cinema. Aoife had told her their chat needed to be more private than usual. It was too important to be picked up by the nosy but well-meaning Lorcan who tended to hover whenever Aoife paid a visit.

She hurried along, hands beneath her armpits for warmth. Despite her gloves, her fingers held the chill of the frost that coated the grassy hills and verges. The clouds seemed to hang heavy in the grey sky, as if they would drop at any moment, crashing down to ruin the world.

Like that bombshell she'd overhead had ruined hers.

She rushed up the short track that led to the farmhouse, her steps firmer now she was almost there, determination and courage filling her, eclipsing the shock somewhat. Caoimhe must have been watching for her, as the front door opened, and the woman stood on the step, her arms folded, perhaps to ward off the nip in the air. Aoife pushed on, desperate to talk now she'd seen her. To let it all out. To relieve herself of the burden. Share it with the one woman she shared everything with.

I can't get through this without her. She'll know what tae do.

"Come away in," Caoimhe said, still blocking the doorway. "I've been so worried about ye after that phone call earlier. What the devil's gone on?"

Aoife's teeth chattered. "It's awful. Feckin' awful."

"Why didn't ye come here last night when ye'd shut the pub? Ah, don't tell me. Patrick would have asked questions. So why didn't ye get ye arse here this mornin' while he's tendin' tae the bar?"

"I needed time tae think. Let me in, for feck's sake. I'm freezin'."

In the warm kitchen, Aoife took her outerwear off and draped it over a spare wooden chair. She sat at the pine table, and although Lorcan and the boys wouldn't be back for some time, Caoimhe still closed the door out of habit. She poured tea from her ancient, cracked-glaze brown teapot, then brought the cups, milk, and sugar over.

She sat, shoving a tin of biscuits across. Aoife ignored them. She couldn't stomach breakfast or lunch earlier and certainly didn't want a custard bloody cream.

Caoimhe sighed. "Tell me, so."

Aoife pulled a cup towards her, wrapping her hands around it to thaw her frigid fingers. Where to begin? "It's tae do wid Tadhg."

"Jaysus Christ, Aoife, didn't I *say* goin' wid him would bring trouble? I'm worried Niamh and Patrick will find out, so I am."

"Niamh likely will before long."

"Shite, what's happened?"

"He's been seein' someone else as well as me. I had no feckin' clue. And she's pregnant."

Caoimhe slapped a hand to her chest. "*What?*"

"Hmm."

"Who?"

"Úna Clancy."

"Oh my feckin' good God. Her man's goin' tae skin her alive; Arlo's not one tae take this lyin' down, we both know that. What the hell's she playin' at? Has she got a death wish? And

Niamh's goin' tae be heartbroken with Rowan only bein' a baby."

"I shouldn't have done it either. Shouldn't have believed him, all those empty promises. What a bloody fool." Aoife drank some tea. "I'm strugglin' wid my emotions. How can I be upset Tadhg's been muckin' around wid Úna when I'm doin' the same behind Patrick's back? I've got no right tae be up in arms about it, yet I am."

"Because ye thought ye had somethin' good wid Tadhg and ye were goin' tae run off together. Wasn't that what he told ye?"

"Ye know it is."

"Then he's a bastard. He was usin' ye. Finish it wid him and pretend it never happened. He's not worth even spittin' on. How did ye find out about this? Earwiggin' as usual, were ye? Haven't ye heard the sayin'? Eavesdroppers never hear good about themselves or however the feck it goes?"

Aoife nodded. She'd heard it all right and a lot more besides. More than she'd ever wanted to know. "He was tellin' Sean Doyle at the bar."

Caoimhe rolled her eyes and sucked in a sharp breath. "Of all the people he could have told, Sean is the worst of it. Do ye think Tadhg told him about ye two as well?"

"I don't know."

"Then we'll pray he hasn't. And if he has, deny it. Patrick will go mad if he finds out. Ye know what he's like about stayin' true."

"He'd shout and rave, but he'd never hit me."

"He might leave ye. Or he'd more likely kick ye out so ye'd have tae go back and live above the pub. Back tae ye daddy."

Aoife winced. Her father was a good man, but she loved her independence, the privacy of living with Patrick, although she wished she'd never agreed to marry him now. She'd gone with Tadhg because her life with Patrick hadn't turned out how she'd hoped. Patrick, moody and sullen since they'd taken their vows, had squashed any happiness they'd had together, flicked the switch that had dimmed her light. She'd dreamed of the perfect marriage but hadn't received it, hadn't got what had been displayed on the tin. She sometimes thought he'd only got together with her because the Fiddler's would come her way when Daddy died. Mammy was long gone, off with the angels, and her father's health had been on the decline when Patrick had asked her on that first date.

He'd used her, she could see that now. Maybe, subconsciously, that's why she hadn't minded having an affair. If he didn't truly care about her, she didn't have to care about him, conveniently brushing any guilt aside.

"Ye're wrong about him leavin' or kickin' me out. He wouldn't let me go even if I admitted it tae him," Aoife whispered. "He has his eye on the pub, and nothin' will stop him from gettin' it, even me pissin' around wid Tadhg. He'd hate what I've done, likely wouldn't touch me again wid a barge pole, and that will be my penance, although him never touchin' me again would be a godsend. I should never have married him, like Niamh should never have married Tadhg. We were both strung a line, promised the world, and neither of us got it."

"It's a sorry mess, so it is. But think on this: there's only Tadhg's word against yours. Those fumbles in the cellar weren't witnessed. Ye told the staff ye were cleanin' the pipes, right?"

"I did."

"And ye're convinced no one knows Tadhg went down there after ye?"

"Yes."

"Then no one can prove it. Patrick was upstairs in the flat, watchin' telly. Sure, he's none the wiser. With it possibly comin' out about Úna bein' pregnant, if Sean pipes up that ye were seein' Tadhg as well, ye can say it's a load of old blarney, alkie talk. Besides, Sean might keep quiet about all of it. Úna might have the baby, palm it off as Arlo's."

Aoife squirmed. Drank some tea. "I haven't told ye all of what I heard."

"Oh feck, woman. What is it? Don't be givin' me a heart attack now."

"Úna's after tellin' Arlo so he'll leave her, which is why Tadhg was panickin' last night. He promised tae run off wid *her*, too. Now she wants him to stick tae his word. She wants away from Arlo, wife beater that he is."

Caoimhe shook her head. "There's goin' tae be ructions."

"There is."

Caoimhe pressed her fingers to her forehead. "Let me think for a minute."

Aoife sipped her tea. Waited for Caoimhe to come up with a solution that would work for everyone. She'd always got Aoife out of scrapes as they'd been growing up, covering for her, supplying lies that had become firm truths, but Aoife worried that this time, no amount of lying would work, not for Tadhg. But Aoife? Yes, she could put any ramblings from Sean down to Tadhg spouting bullshit, and she'd be safe from a Patrick rant that would go on for weeks, maybe even months and, if she remained with him forever, the rest of her life. Patrick was good at holding grudges, and he'd remind her of her transgression every chance he got.

Could she stand that? Did she even *want* to stay with Patrick? No. If she did, she wouldn't have messed about with Tadhg. If she loved her husband, truly, it would never have entered her head to have sex with another man in the cold beer cellar in the first place.

"Okay," Caoimhe said. "The only option is ye lie through the back teeth about havin' anythin' tae do with Tadhg. Even if he outright says it in front of ye and Patrick, ye don't buckle. Then ye stay with Patrick for as long as ye can manage, showin' the village ye're devoted to him, and maybe, in years tae come, ye might find ye're happy tae be with him. Or ye can go ye separate ways. When all of this is forgotten."

"It'll never be forgotten, not in Caldraich."

"No, but it'll fade. Shite like this will be swept under the rug eventually. No one will want tae talk out loud about an affair baby, for the child's sake." Caoimhe sat straighter. "I know what else we can do."

"What?"

Caoimhe got up and reached for the landline phone hanging on the wall. "We'll get Úna over here."

Aoife's stomach rolled over. But she nodded.

Feck.

Chapter Twenty-Nine

The Feud – Part Two

She had kept her mouth shut like Caoimhe and Aoife had asked. It was a sensible plan all round. Despite Úna reeling on the day Caoimhe had phoned her, asking her to go to the Sullivan farm, and Úna wanting revenge, to put Tadhg in his place and force him to take her away from

Caldraich to England like he'd promised, she knew it would be useless.

Because Aoife had passed on a nasty snippet she'd overheard. That Tadhg had no *intention* of leaving Niamh, never had, so no amount of forcing would have got Úna what she wanted. The tapestry of supposed love he'd woven had come undone, loose threads all over the place, all tangled in a jumble. As they'd sat around drinking tea, hashing it out, Úna had realised her dreams of a better life, away from Arlo, who regularly beat her, ruled her, weren't going to come to fruition.

So for all those long, anxious months of her pregnancy, fretting whether the baby would look like Tadhg, dark-haired instead of blonde like Úna and Arlo, she'd remained quiet about her affair. About Aoife and Tadhg's. No one needed to know he'd been seeing *another* woman behind Úna's and Niamh's backs. It would muddy the waters, although a part of Úna would relish the villagers seeing him in a stark, disgusting light. A philanderer, someone not to be trusted around women. But then wasn't that the same for Úna and Aoife? Neither of them could be trusted either, tarts that they were.

Except Úna wasn't a tart, not really. She'd fallen for Tadhg's charm, his lies, yearning for that pot of gold at the end of an English rainbow. All she'd wanted was a chance to escape to the UK. And she'd *loved* Tadhg, loved him something rotten, yet he'd blabbed to Sean and ruined everything.

Too many people knew what Úna and done, albeit her friends, the secret trysts that had lived inside a secret pocket exposed now. Guilt and fear had meant she'd lost weight, drawing concern from the midwife, Keavy. Paranoia was a constant. She imagined whispers when there weren't any, sidelong glances that didn't exist, worrying that Sean had been spreading gossip, telling people to keep it away from Úna's, Arlo's, and Niamh's ears but "Feel free to chat about it amongst yourselves!" People in Caoimhe were good at knowing everything yet acting as if they knew nothing. She'd been a party to keeping gossip quiet while going over it again and again with others in the know.

It wasn't so amusing when the tables were turned, her the source of entertainment.

She trusted Caoimhe and Aoife—especially Aoife, who had a vested interest in keeping everything under wraps—and didn't for one minute think they'd open their mouths, but as for Sean…

A few months ago, Úna had toyed with visiting him, begging him not to say anything, but as the initial days after going to Caoimhe's had worn on, she'd concluded—or hoped—he didn't plan to say *anything*. Perhaps he was a better friend to Tadhg than she'd thought. Perhaps Tadhg had expressed how important it was for this not to get out. After all, Niamh's family down in Cork were a frightening bunch, so she'd always said, and if they found out, they'd come up here and do some damage to Tadhg, even to Sean just for knowing about it. Tadhg wouldn't want the shame, and Sean wouldn't want his precious good looks ruined. Plus there was his wife, Erin, who'd be furious if the Cork lot turned up on her doorstep. The Doyles had too many fingers in too many pies for them to have trouble marching in and letting fists fly. She wouldn't want the attention that would bring to her scheming family.

She'd likely told Sean to zip his lips or else.

Úna stared down at the baby she'd pushed out of her womb a couple of hours ago. No hospital for her, she'd wanted a home birth—the less people who saw what the child looked like the better. The midwife had gone, and Úna was alone with the wee scrap she'd kept hidden inside her for nine months. Arlo, at work, had refused to stay home today to be by her side. He wasn't one for doing *anything* if he didn't want to. Said birthing was women's business.

Tiny Saoirse was the image of Tadhg, hair black as night.

Úna's eyes stung, and her stomach cramped with fear. She had four hours before Arlo came back, so she had time to run away instead of having to face her husband and taking the one beating she thought she deserved. For her deception—not only an affair but praying she could pass this child off as his.

She placed a sleeping Saoirse in the Moses basket and shuffled off to the bathroom. Took a quick shower and fitted sanitary pads in her knickers, two wide, another poking up the back. She didn't know how long she'd be on the road. There might not be that many toilets along the way where she could stop and sort herself out.

She dressed, packed a suitcase, cramming in as many baby clothes and nappies as she could, leaving herself only three outfits. She squeezed in a bottle and a tin of formula in case Saoirse didn't take to the breast in the days to come, although she'd latched on fine after the birth.

Úna couldn't rely on nature. She had to be able to feed her little one, the only grand thing to come out of all this.

A knock at the door stilled her as she was about to zip the case up. Keavy was a lip-flapping middle-aged woman who'd probably gone off to the Fiddler's for her lunch and mentioned Saoirse's entrance into this mad and worrying world.

Úna collected her baby, swaddled her in a blanket so her hair wasn't on show, and went downstairs. Opened the door.

Niamh.

Oh feck. No, this can't be happening.

"Ah, so I've not long seen Keavy down the road there." Niamh smiled. "Ye've had the baby, so ye have. I know what it's like tae birth at home and not have your man there, so I've come tae help." She glanced at six-month-old Rowan asleep in his pushchair beside her. "He looks like a big old monster compared tae ye new one." She laughed and gave Úna her attention again. "Well, out of the way wid ye, then!"

Stunned, and confused, and not knowing what to do, Úna stepped back. Niamh expertly brought the pushchair over the step and wheeled it into the kitchen. Úna closed the door, her heart hammering, her legs still weak from labour.

I'll get rid of her after a cup of tea.

She joined the woman who'd taken off her coat and rolled up her sleeves, presumably to tackle last night's washing up in the sink. Úna had been having contractions since she and Arlo had eaten, and he'd slept on through the night while she'd paced downstairs, waiting for her waters to break. He'd breezed off to work this morning, uncaring that her pains were coming three minutes apart.

It wasn't a surprise for Niamh to get stuck in and clean up the mess. The women of Caldraich still lived to old-time rules in some respects, and if someone had a baby, it was expected the neighbours would help out.

If only Keavy hadn't opened her big mouth.

Úna should have known someone down this street would have spotted the midwife leaving. Niamh was one of the kindest people around, and the most respectful, so she'd clearly waited a short time after Keavy had left to come and offer her services, and her busy with a baby herself.

Guilt poked Úna hard in the chest. She should never have tried to steal this woman's husband. But her desperate need to leave her life with Arlo, and Tadhg's supposed love for her, had erased all of her morals.

"Let me have a quick looksee, then I'll get on wid the housework." Niamh sat at the table and held her arms out.

She's goin' tae see her face. Her hair. She's goin' tae know.

Úna had long since thought up an excuse for the black hair—her uncle on her mother's side was dark when all his siblings were fair.

But what if he was an affair baby, too?

Against her better judgement, and perhaps subconsciously she wanted to test whether anyone would comment on Saoirse's appearance, Úna passed the bundle over. Niamh stared down at the tiny face, her smile fading, then she peeled the blanket back from around the head. Sucked in a sharp breath. Peered over at Rowan.

"Ye know, I always thought Tadhg had been seein' other women, but I never thought ye'd be one of them. I thought..." Niamh's laugh sounded choked. "I thought ye had more respect for me than that."

She glanced up, and the tears in her eyes broke Úna's heart, her soul, and brought all the guilt tumbling back.

"She's the spit of him and Rowan." Niamh gazed down at the baby again. "What a beautiful little girl. Sadly, I don't think ye're goin' tae get away wid it, love. Arlo—"

"I was runnin' away before ye came. I wanted...I didn't want tae put ye through anythin', and I didn't want a beatin' when Arlo saw her. I'm so sorry. Tadhg is..."

"Aye, I know what Tadhg is, I'm just sad *ye* didn't. He's out for all he can get, any way he can, a stór."

Úna, shocked that Niamh had called her 'darling' despite everything, sank to a chair, hot tears brimming then falling. "He said we'd go tae England, start a new life. But when I told him I was pregnant, he stopped seein' me. I found out he'd lied, that he was seein' someone else as well and had told her the same thing."

Niamh looked up sharply. "Who?"

"I can't tell ye that."

Niamh nodded. "This bloody village and it's rules on secrets. How many people know?"

Úna totted it up in her head. Aoife, Caoimhe, Sean. "Other than me and Tadhg, three. And they wouldn't have known if he hadn't opened his big, drunk mouth."

"Ah, his secrets always come out when he's in his cups, but then again, he's never outright admitted tae me he sleeps around. How did it go down?"

"He told someone about the pregnancy, in the pub, and a customer overheard. They told someone else who then told me." Úna wasn't about to give names, hence saying 'customer' instead of Aoife, nor would she put Caoimhe in the firing line. "Two of them won't breathe a word, I can promise ye that, but as for the other one…"

"It'll be Sean Doyle. Thick as thieves, those two. I don't think he'd blab either, so ye're safe."

Úna gawped at her. "So ye're not goin' tae say anythin'?"

Niamh tutted. "And have the shame of people knowin' my husband fathered another woman's child? Havin' my family know down in Cork? Affairs are one thing, but a baby? That's a step too far. It's not a good idea for me tae kick him out, milseán."

"Why are ye callin' me sweetheart when I've been such a bitch tae ye?"

Niamh wiped tears that had fallen down her cheeks. "Because I know what it feels like tae be wid a man who hits ye."

Úna reeled from those words. Her skin turned clammy from a flush of heat. How could she have got it so wrong? *Him* so wrong? Niamh went about as if she had the happiest of marriages, yet…

But didn't ye do the same? Hidin' it? Pretendin' tae the world it wasn't happenin'?

"He's a liar," Niamh said. "He says whatever he can tae get ye in the bed."

"Why…why haven't ye left him?"

Niamh scoffed. "My family are staunch Catholics. They warned me not tae marry a Protestant man, but I didn't listen. I met him in Cork, he was on a stag do. We had a whirlwind romance that weekend, and I ran tae Caldraich weeks later after his phone calls, thinkin' he was my feckin' knight. He was for a while…"

"The same wid me and Arlo. The knight thing."

"Bastards, the pair of them." Niamh gazed down at Saoirse. "Where will ye go?"

"I don't know."

A knock on the door startled them both.

"It'll be another of the neighbours, so it will." Niamh tutted and handed the baby back. "I'll answer it. Tell them I'm dealin' wid things for ye."

Úna watched her go. Clutched her newborn to her chest and wished she'd had the guts to go and see a friend in Liverpool so she could have had an abortion in secret. But she was so attached to her child now and was glad she'd had her.

Niamh's strident voice coming through from the front door snapped Úna out of her past mistakes and straight back into the current one — she should never have let Niamh in.

"What are ye doin' here?" Niamh snapped.

"Um…err…what are *ye* doin' here?" Tadhg.

Oh feck. Oh no…

"I've come tae look after the mother, so I have. It's what we do. Are ye goin' tae tell me ye skipped out of work tae come and collect Arlo for wettin' the baby's head? He's not here. I expect she went through it on her own."

"I…"

"*Tsk*. Come in and see your new child," Niamh said.

"What?"

"Ye heard me. And put the door on the chain in case Arlo bothers tae come back. We can at least get fair warnin'."

Úna stared at the kitchen doorway.

Niamh appeared, going to sit in her seat, shaking her head at Úna, perhaps to warn her not to say anything. "We'll sort it between us three, all right? Come tae an agreement. I'm not puttin' up wid his shite anymore."

Tadhg walked in, his face flushed. "I…"

"Sit down," Niamh barked.

Tadhg gave her a dark look.

Niamh laughed. "Those days are over, ye bastard fecker. I won't be cowerin' from ye anymore. I swear tae God, if ye touch me one more time, I'll get on tae my brothers, and they'll be up here like a shot tae sort ye out. This baby, she's yours, but ye will *not* tell anyone that. *I* will not tell anyone. *Úna* will not tell anyone. To everyone else, she's Arlo's. The black hair is a throwback or some such shite. What we'll do when she grows up and looks even more like ye and Rowan I don't know, but for now, we play the game." She stared at Úna. "How bad is Arlo tae ye?"

"He'll kill me."

"Right, so if he was dead ye wouldn't lose any sleep?"

Úna swallowed. "No. I hate him."

"Then my brothers will come tonight. They'll sort him, so they will. He won't be a problem anymore. He'll be gone for good, just like Tadhg will if he so much as lays one finger on me again." She glared at her husband. "Keep Arlo out all evenin'. Get him pissed up. My brothers will need time tae make the journey."

Úna glanced at Tadhg, but he wouldn't look at her. He gazed at Saoirse, then Rowan, shaking his head. Siblings sleeping in tandem, children who'd never know they were related.

Niamh broke the silence. "As for us three, we'll never speak again. We had a row, here, today, and we couldn't resolve our differences—there's a feud, that's the only option for us tae get away wid this. It means no Ahearn will speak tae a Clancy anymore and vice versa. Families stick by their own, take up the feud despite not knowin' what the feck it's about. That's just the way it is. No one will ask questions about what the feud is, ye know how it goes in this village; people accept there's been a barney and sit back tae watch the atmosphere change when rowing families walk in the Fiddler's." Niamh glared at Tadhg. "Ye will *not* see Úna again, Úna will *not* see ye. *I'm* the boss in the house now, not ye. Understand? Otherwise, ye'll be treated the same as Arlo."

Tadhg lowered his head. Walked out. The tinkle of the chain came, then the slam of the door.

"See what a bastard he is?" Niamh asked. "He slammed that feckin' door and didn't care that he might wake the babies."

"Arlo…"

Niamh's expression changed to one that Úna imagined had lived on her face in Cork, when she'd been a part of her family, one that ran around ruling the roost like the Doyles. She'd got out of that life, thinking the one in Northern Ireland would be better, and it wasn't. She'd clearly been cowed by Tadhg, and God help him now she'd slipped back into her old skin.

Niamh glowered. "I'm goin' back tae havin' a backbone. I won't lie down and take whatever my husband dishes out. As for Arlo… Ye've just had a baby, no one will suspect ye of doin' anythin' tae him. Keep her head covered if he comes in, although, if Tadhg knows what's good for him, he'll wait for Arlo after work and take him straight tae the pub. When the garda come, ye act shocked."

Úna blinked at the information overload, how swiftly this was happening. "Why are ye doin' this? Why get so involved?"

"Because I've remembered my reputation is everythin' tae me. I won't have my family knowin' what a shite state I've made of my life." Niamh stood, took hold of the pushchair handle, and wheeled her son towards the kitchen door. "I'm sorry my husband did this tae ye. So bloody sorry. And I'll be sad not bein' able tae speak tae ye anymore, but it's for the best."

Then she left.

Úna stood on wobbly legs, Arlo's fate something she couldn't alter now—she didn't even want to. She was a party to an upcoming murder and, saddened that she'd lose Niamh's friendship over the fake feud, she accepted it *was* for the best. She'd have a job on her hands, watching Saoirse and Rowan growing up together, if she stayed. But she could hardly skip town now, and not tomorrow either, not when Arlo would turn up dead.

That was a problem for another day. For now, she'd do the washing up.

Chapter Thirty

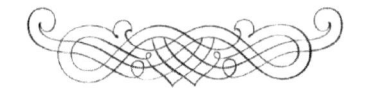

Rowan couldn't stand seeing Saoirse and not being able to speak with her. She'd come back from the UK looking drawn and upset. No wonder, she'd just given up her baby. The idea that she'd felt pushed into doing it, be it because of a feud or her morals, hurt Rowan's heart. They could have made it work. Could have run away and started again. No one in the UK would shame them for having a child out of wedlock

like those in the village. Sometimes, their out-dated views got on his nerves, but he understood them and why they couldn't seem to shake them off.

She'd never had another man since. He'd never had another woman. For years, the pair of them had remained true to one another, even though they couldn't have a relationship. Why, though?

Feck it, he was going to talk to her. See if she knew why the hell they couldn't be together. Mammy wouldn't talk about it, which was usual for Caldraich feuds, but God, he was her son and wouldn't say anything to an outsider.

He and Saoirse had always known they were playing with fire. Sneaking around to see each other, worrying if they'd be seen. Ahearns and Clancys had never given each other the time of day for as far back as he could remember. But Rowan and Saoirse had gone to school together, and as little kids they hadn't known to stay apart. Until one day Mammy had said he couldn't go near her anymore, that he'd be going against his family if he did. At eight years old, he'd gathered the importance of that, how family was the be all and end all, so he'd done as she'd asked.

Years later, a few shy glances later, and Rowan had slipped Saoirse a note in the Fiddler's as he'd walked past to go to the men's. She'd met him in the back yard, breathless and excited to be called outside. They'd talked, skirting around the feud at first, then had discussed it, agreeing that what had gone on in the past shouldn't dictate their lives.

The romance had been born.

Rowan sipped his pint of lager, glancing across at her like in the old days when they'd had a certain look to say they should meet out the back. She nodded from her seat at the table by the fire and drank her drink. She sat with two of her friends who were shrieking and laughing at something or other.

Rowan got up and left the bar, the corridor to the rear door seeming a mile away. Outside, he stood against the wall of the building so the security light didn't snap on, a trick both of them had employed in the past. Hands in pockets so he didn't bite his nails, he waited. And waited.

The soft click of the door being opened had him turning to see if she came out. Aoife wasn't averse to nipping here for a sneaky cigarette, a habit she claimed she didn't partake in. But Saoirse stepped out and stood right beside him.

"Are ye okay?" he whispered.

"As okay as I can be."

"The baby..."

"It was…hard. I didn't want tae do it, but Mammy said it was for the best, considerin'."

"Considerin' what? Did ye find out what the feud was?"

"I did."

"And ye didn't tell *me? All this time?"*

"Ye know the rules."

"But surely ye could have let me know. I've been goin' crazy, wonderin' what's so bad that we can't be together."

"It's bad. Ye should ask ye mammy."

"She won't let on. She's stubborn. She'd keep secrets beyond the grave, that one."

"It's somethin' I think ye should know. Ye deserve tae know. It knocked me for six, so it did."

"Look, I'm never goin' tae be told. If I deserve tae be in the know, just feckin' say it quick. If it's quick, it means ye never said it at all."

He imagined her smiling in the dark at that. It was something they'd always said to each other in the early days, both of them too nervous to express their feelings, love and all that went with it a maze to navigate. If the other didn't want to deal with what had been said, they pretended it didn't exist to save their blushes.

"Ye're my brother."

She walked inside, a choked sob inserting itself between two of his ragged exhales. He moved to go after her then stopped. She couldn't handle discussing it further, she had to remove herself, and he wouldn't force her to expand on what she'd said. His mind whirled, confusion and disbelief warring inside him. Was Mammy not his Mammy? Was Úna? Had she given him up to Daddy? No, how could she be? There wasn't enough time between their birthdays for Úna to have had two pregnancies that close together. So it was Daddy who'd cheated with Úna and Saoirse was the result.

No wonder there had been a feud. Jaysus Christ.

He took a deep breath and entered the pub. Went back to his pint, which he drank as calmly as he could, although his hand shook. He cast a quick glance to Saoirse's table. She sat stony-faced, and her red-rimmed eyes told the story. He wanted to comfort her. She caught his gaze, mouthed, "I love you," and then turned away.

He loved her, too, but it would now have to switch to a brotherly love, a hidden one at that, a love he couldn't show, not if the secret had to be kept and the feud maintained. His father stood talking to an old-timer in Sean's absence, and Rowan had to fight not to go over there and ask that all-important question.

He finished his drink and lifted a hand in farewell to Aoife who gave him a funny look, then she switched her attention to Saoirse.

Aoife swung her gaze back to Rowan. "Oh God. Don't do it, lad."

She'd twigged.

He nodded to say he wouldn't breathe a word. Strolled out as if he didn't have a heavy weight on his mind. So Aoife knew, she was in on it. Just what the feck had happened for her to be involved?

He jogged home, already thinking about Ichabod and London, getting the hell out of here so he could distance himself from this. From Saoirse, the love of his life. God had played a mean trick and no mistake. He slid the key in the lock and opened the door, the familiar scent of their house smacking into him. He'd miss that. He shut the door and found his mother in the kitchen, cleaning up after the dinner they'd had not an hour ago. She'd shooed Rowan and Daddy to the pub, saying she needed a bit of peace.

Rowan sat at the table. "So Saoirse is my sister, eh?"

Mammy dropped a plate into the bowl, suds flying, water splashing. She didn't look at him, instead staring at her reflection in the window above the sink. What did she see? A liar? Did she hate herself for whatever part she'd played in this mess? "Who told ye?"

"Saoirse herself. Her mammy had the decency tae let her know. Likely because of the baby." *He hadn't thought of the issues of that until now. Would it have been born with something wrong with it because they were siblings? He'd have loved it to death anyway, but there was no point in thinking about could-have-beens.*

"Now ye see it was for the best."

"I do, but it would have been nice tae have had it explained tae me instead of bein' left in the dark. Still, it's done now. Who are her parents?"

"Ye daddy and Úna."

"So he played away, even though the Cork family would have beaten the shite out of him for it?"

"Tadhg believed he could do whatever he wanted, includin' beatin' me."

That shocked the shite out of him. "What?"

"He doesn't do that anymore. Hasn't touched me since the day Saoirse was born."

"So this is the reason for the feud?"

"No, the feud doesn't exist. We made one up."

"Why?"

"Because I couldn't allow those two tae speak tae each other. A pretend feud was better, one none of us would talk about."

"Ye didn't want tae rip Úna's hair out and kick Daddy tae the kerb?"

"Yes regardin' ye daddy, but that wouldn't have solved anythin'. But I hold no anger towards Úna, never did. She was tricked; Tadhg had a silver tongue. He promised her the world. And Aoife."

"Aoife? Jaysus! What a bastard."

"We promised we'd never tell anyone, so don't go speakin' tae him. Let it lie, son."

He stood. "I love ye for bein' so kind tae Úna, I'd expect nothin' less of ye, but I'll be leavin' for London in the mornin'."

"Ichabod's settin' ye up, I take it?"

"He will."

"Don't tell him."

Rowan left the room and went upstairs to pack, his eyes burning. He wanted to kill Daddy for what he'd done. He hauled a holdall down from the top of his wardrobe, and the too-late realisation that he'd had sex with his sister barrelled into him. But they hadn't known, they'd been innocent in all this, so he was damned if he'd allow that burden to travel with him all the way to the UK.

Sometimes, secrets weren't best kept, they should be told — before anyone developed intimate feelings.

He sat on the bed, the bag beside him, and typed in a message.

Rowan: I've found out what went on. Coming to London tomorrow, tell you then.

Ichabod: Shite. Is it bad?

Rowan: Worse than ye'd imagine.

Ichabod: I'll get hold of my bosses now. They'll find something for you. Maybe set you up in their new casino.

Rowan: I owe you.

Ichabod: I owe you, too, remember.

The Doyles. That family hadn't been seen for a long time, and people had assumed they'd moved away, considering Patrick's body parts had been found on the hills. They'd come to the conclusion the Doyles had killed Patrick then scarpered. No one in Caldraich gave much of a toss where they were, although there had been shock at finding out Patrick was dead. Aoife, though, either she was hiding her grief regarding her husband or she didn't care either. She'd remained stoic ever since, not wanting to talk about it. Tommy had periodically knocked at the Doyles' door but never got an answer. Shay had headed the investigation as to where they'd gone and he'd eventually gone into the house, finding no sign of them. Their phones had been tracked to Liverpool, so they must have taken the ferry. At that point, they'd been switched off.

Rowan knew the true story. Ichabod had called him after he'd been to see some man called Solly in London. At least one of his family members trusted him enough with secrets. Weird, though, how Shay hadn't noticed the smell of rotting bodies in the loft.

Or he hadn't said he had anyway.

Maybe he was more bent than they thought. In deep with the drug gang.

Rowan rose and got on with packing his bag.

A new life waited for him across the sea.

Chapter Thirty-One

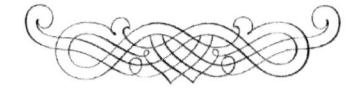

George smiled grimly when the North London leader answered the phone with a chirpy, "George! How the fucking fuck are you?" He had to play this the right way. Much as he wanted to bark at the tosser for deceiving them, the main objective had to remain at the top of his priority list.

"I'm all right, Solly. You?"

"Brilliant, you cunt, brilliant. To what do I owe this honour?"

"That drink…"

"Fuck me, that was ages ago we were supposed to arrange that."

"Been busy, mate."

"For years?"

"You know how it is."

"I do, so I won't hold it against you, fuckface."

George clenched his teeth to concentrate on that rather than the rising anger. "You could have reminded me at any of the leader meetings."

"There is that, yeah, but so could you. Anyway, busy, so…when and where?" Solly asked.

"Tonight, our pub, the Noodle and Tiger."

"Ah, I've heard good things about that place."

I bet you have. An ideal corner to peddle drugs.

George had already caught a teenager loitering. He'd sent him off with a gentle flea in his ear, not mentioning Solly in case the kid went back and told him. It could have served as a warning to get the gear out of Cardigan, and he didn't want that. "Eight o'clock all right?"

"Yeah, yeah. See you later."

George stared at his phone screen then turned to Greg in the driver's seat. "I don't know about you, but I'm chuffing knackered. It's been a long day."

"A quick nap before we go and see that wanker?"

"Hmm. Home, James."

Greg tutted. "Fuck off. I've told you about that before. I am *not* your driver, cockwomble."

As always, the pub buzzed with people, the smell in the air a mix of the various cut-price meals on offer. George was tempted to have a Pot Noodle and tiger bread, but they'd arranged to meet Ichabod later at the Taj for a curry—after Solly and Daggers had been dealt with. Mason had found out where the drug dealer lived and stood when selling. He currently haunted Katy's street for some reason, Mason sitting in his car, watching him. George didn't plan to hang about with the other leader once they got to the warehouse, pricking around by providing a meal before they shot the bloke, a last supper—he wanted a quick interrogation then execution.

He entered the pub, Greg on his heels, and scanned the area. Solly sat with Bonce on a dais, a bottle of champagne on the table with four glasses. Solly was a showman, always flaunting his wealth—some of that wealth gained from selling on Cardigan without permission, which grated on George's, Mad George's, and Ruffian's nerves. With all three of his selves annoyed about it, he'd have a hard time containing his anger.

"The other two are knocking," he whispered to Greg, meaning Mad and Ruffian.

"Fuck. Tell them to piss off for now."

They approached the dais, George talking to his alters in his head.

"Bog off. You're not needed here."

"But it's the lying that gets me," Mad said. *"He fucking bullshitted all of you. He'll die quickly from being shot. Can't we torture him? Use the medieval tools?"*

"No. I mean it. Fuck off." He climbed the steps and sat at the table opposite the two men who had their backs to the wall. George usually sat like that, he didn't like not seeing who was coming in, but he'd have to suck it up. "All right, Solly?"

Greg sat beside him. "Evening."

Solly nodded a greeting. "Pour, Bonce."

Bonce obeyed, like the creepy wanker he was, filling the glasses halfway. Despite not wanting to, George raised his to tap it against the others being held up, telling himself it was a toast to Solly's death.

"To being best mates!" Solly declared.

Jesus wept…

"Yeah." George smiled. "And because we're best mates, I've got a proposition for you. Lucrative. We don't trust anyone else, hence why we decided to approach you about it."

Solly deflated. "So this is a business meeting, not a matey knees-up."

"That and a catch-up."

The man brightened. "Right. I was gonna say… Drink up, the night is young."

They chatted shit for a while, Bonce clearly memorising everything. Then George brought up the subject of an alliance regarding the sale of guns. Solly nodded eagerly and couldn't seem to get enough of it. Even Bonce appeared more animated. Was this geezer a right-hand man to the degree he persuaded Solly to do things? Things he shouldn't, as per leader law?

"Millions are in the offing," George said. "Pounds, that is."

Solly's eyes widened. "I'm in. Where are the goods?"

George leaned forward to whisper, "Our warehouse for now, but we're carting them to our secret location later." He wouldn't say where that was, a hidden room in Under the Dryer, a hairdressing salon they used as one of their business fronts. But there were no guns for sale and they weren't going anywhere.

"Let's go." Solly rose, swigging the rest of his champers. "We'll follow you."

The street stood empty, the other leaders likely parking elsewhere. A line of their cars would have alerted Solly as to what was going on. The same as with Goldie, they weren't going to give the bloke a heads-up, although Goldie had been lured in knowing other leaders would be there. George had sent Evan the keycode to let everyone in, which he'd change once this was all over.

He opened up the warehouse and thought about telling Bonce to make himself scarce, but the man would have to be collateral damage, seeing as he knew Solly was here. He couldn't run bleating to other leaders about his boss' murder, and besides, even if they weren't in on this they wouldn't give a fuck about what he had to say, but he might well do an anonymous tip-off to the police.

"Gentlemen first," George said in the little square hallway. He held his arm out for Solly and Bonce to go in before him.

"Ah, is this a surprise gathering?" Solly asked upon seeing the other leaders.

"No," George said in his ear, pausing before he used one of the names Solly liked to call people. "It's the last day of your life, you cunt."

Chapter Thirty-Two

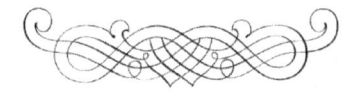

Daggers had received a message from Katy Marlborough. She'd apparently been in the loo in an Italian restaurant, although what the fuck he'd needed to know that for he wasn't sure. She'd secured someone to run the business for her now Josephine was dead. Katy's message had been rude as fuck. She needed a bit of leeway on what Josephine owed him, plus she'd had the cheek to ask for more gear on tick. If he didn't agree, she knew a man who'd make him.

Daggers didn't like threats. Not towards him anyway. He'd replied that he'd think about it, but instead he'd shaken his head at her audacity and wouldn't think about it at all. Then today, he'd been asking around about her. Someone had told him her address, so he'd visited her street and spoken to her neighbours. She was a tart, plain and simple. A money-grabber at that. No one knew what she did for a living, although she *had* been striking up conversations lately about antiques, trying to sell them. Maybe that was to cover her sister's debts. He'd like to think so but wouldn't hold his breath.

He hadn't seen her at all today from his perch on the street sign at the corner. He'd been peddling drugs while he was at it, never one to stay idle if there was money to be made. He'd need more product soon and had messaged Mr Weed but so far hadn't received a response. He was annoyed at Josephine because he'd paid Mr Weed what she owed out of his own takings, and now she owed Daggers. Well, she didn't, Katy did.

"Where the fuck is she?"

It was late, dark, and he'd been here for hours. Some big bloke in a baseball cap with a long beard and hair shuffled past, maybe a tramp, going by the state of his baggy, grubby clothes. Even in the light of a lamppost it was easy to see the fella was down on his uppers. He had sunglasses on, which was weird at night.

Maybe he was blind.

"You should have one of those white sticks," Daggers called after him.

The man stopped just as a small white van pulled up. He turned to face Daggers. Walked towards him. "Whuh?"

Jesus. He can't even speak properly. Has he lost his teeth?

"I said, you should get one of those white sticks," Daggers shouted.

A whack to the back of his head sent him to his knees. He registered being dragged, the van engine no longer rumbling, and whispers.

"In here. No one will find him until he stinks." Scottish accent.

"Fuck me, he weighs more than he looks." London accent.

Grunts, more dragging, his heels scraping over the ground. Then they stopped.

A weird noise, like clicking.

"Fucking lock pick's sticking," the Scottish one said. "Ah, there we go."

Hauled inside, he felt what he reckoned was lino beneath his heels. He glanced around, his eyesight so fuzzy from the wallop to his head he could only make out shapes, but he was in one of the houses. Which one? A door closed, and the sounds of bolts drawing across had him shuddering, becoming more alert.

"Woss going on?" he managed.

"We hear you've been selling for Mr Weed on Cardigan."

"So?"

"*So?*" Scottish laughed. "Oh dear, he doesn't care, Greg."

"No, George."

George? Greg? Oh shit. It couldn't be them, could it?

"Mr Weed said it would be all right, that he had a deal with you," Daggers rushed to say, scared out of his mind and wanting this sorted. "If he lied, that's not my fault."

"We're past caring," George said in his normal voice. "Seriously."

They dropped Daggers on the floor.

"Don't go all Mad on this one," Greg said. "We're meant to be at the Taj in an hour. Bloody stupid to have done this now when we're short on time."

"Why waste a good opportunity?"

"W-what are you going to do to me?" Daggers needed a piss. He was that frightened he'd almost done it in his jeans.

"Get rid of you and all the other scumbags who Mr Weed sent to our Estate."

"Ah, come on, man. I've got a kid, innit."

"Don't care. We'll find out who she is, your missus if you have one, and give her some money to bury you. But that could be a while. Katy's dead, and we're in her house. She's got no other family to realise she isn't around, so no one's going to come looking until you start to smell, and even then the neighbours will think it's the drains."

"Unless we take a leaf out of Solly's book," Greg said.

What's that? Who's Solly? Daggers slowly backed away, pushing himself along the floor on his arse. If he could get to the other exit, he'd be free. He couldn't work out if he was at the front or back of the house, though.

"The loft?" George asked then laughed, the grumble of it sinister in the dark. "Might work. I've got a roll of plastic sheeting in the van an' all. Duct tape. The smell wouldn't spread then."

"I'll get it and the suits."

Suits?

Daggers had reached the doorway of whatever room they were in. It was closed, so he was going to have to stand and wrench it open, which would eat up time. Greg walked out, and Daggers caught sight of the night sky and the bobbly tops of hedges. The back garden? Fuck, if he managed to escape, that would mean Greg would see him out the front, unless he had his head stuck in the rear of the van getting that bloody plastic.

"Where the fuck do you think *you're* going?" George asked. He pulled down a blind on the door then the window, blocking the view to outside. He didn't rush, as though he wasn't fussed whether Daggers made a run for it. Like he knew he'd catch him.

But not if I get in the bathroom and lock the door.
Knowing these two, they'll break the door down.

A light snapped on. Daggers blinked, trying to get his eyes used to the brightness quickly. A kitchen, a nice big one, George heading towards him. It was so weird, him with a ginger beard and hair. He'd seen him around the East End, of course he had, but he'd never been this close.

George gripped Daggers' hair and hauled him to his feet. "You're not going anywhere, sunshine."

The back door opened, and the end of a roll of plastic came in first, followed by Greg who dumped it on the floor. He shut the door, bolted it, and bent to tug the loose end of plastic. The roll glided over the floor, creating a large sheet.

"What the fuck have you done that now for?" George asked, giving Daggers' hair a little wrench. "We've got to kill him first."

"No bloodshed. We don't want to give anyone a clue something's up if they look through the window."

"But I've shut the blinds."

"No, we do this my way."

"Fuck's sake. Strangling hurts my hands because it takes so long."

"Then put him in a sleep hold and get a cushion from somewhere. Suffocate the bastard. Sit on his face. Whatever, just get it done."

Daggers' bladder released, a hot stream soaking his jeans.

"Katy had better have a mop and bucket in this place," George said. "The baby's gone and pissed himself."

Chapter Thirty-Three

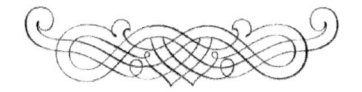

Ichabod patted his stomach, his belly full of curry. The twins hadn't mentioned any reason for this meal other than them winding down after a job well done. Still, he was anxious, waiting for one of them to say something. Or maybe he was imagining the elephant in the room, whatever that may be.

They were at the coffee stage, and Ichabod was glad for the caffeine. He was off to Marleigh's after this. She'd messaged to say her mother had gone home and did he want to pop in for a chat. She'd added that this mess had taught her a sharp lesson: it didn't matter what anyone thought of your life choices so long as it sat right with you.

What was she really saying? That she was prepared to give up her time alone to think about any future relationship with him? He'd have to abide by the rules or morality and say they should still keep their status quiet for a while. Not only did seeing another man so soon after her husband had died seem wrong, crass, the police investigation would be ongoing until all avenues had been exhausted. Mr Weed wouldn't be found to blame the murder on, so Janine might have to keep the case open for longer than they'd like, pretending to look for him. Marleigh would be a suspect no matter whether she'd washed her car and weeded her garden to provide herself with an alibi. Spouses were always inspected closely.

But if she was ready to jump in with him… He could hardly believe it. Months of thinking about her, wishing she was his. Could he accept that might be true now?

"Got something to say to you," George said to break the patch of silence.

Was this it? The praise Ichabod wanted?

"What's that, then?"

"You've been fucking amazing during all this—and before, I might add. We consider you a part of our core team now, top-tier shit, which means more wages and a better place to live. More suits." George smiled.

"Right..."

"So we've been thinking. Rowan's adept at running Jackpot Palace, and we're contemplating getting him to take over your shift and putting someone else in his current position."

"Oh."

"Don't look like that. This is a step up for you."

"Doin' what?"

"As you know, we use Moon's men, Alien and Brickhouse, from time to time because other than Will, Martin, Janine, and Cameron, we don't trust the others on the team quite enough to be with us on the secretive jobs. The nastier ones. Except for you."

Ichabod smiled, chuffed to bits. "Thank ye."

"Seeing your ninja skills in action... Fuck me, you're at a professional level. So we want you on hand immediately if shit hits the fan. As it stands, you have to fuck about getting hold of Rowan to come in before you can leave the casino. This way, you'd only have to leave your pad. Or Marleigh's."

Ichabod smiled, his cheeks growing hot. "I don't know about that yet. I'm goin' tae see her in a bit." He considered what this new job would entail. "What would I do wid my time in between? I'd be bored."

"Surveillance, as usual, and apprehending subjects."

"Can I not work alongside Rowan, still bringin' someone in tae cover his current shift? I can leave at a moment's notice, then. Honestly, I need tae keep busy."

"Because of the Sullivan thing?"

"That and I'm no good tae anyone if I'm left tae my own devices."

"Okay." George's phone rang, and he frowned at the screen. "What does she want?" He answered. "Everything all right, Deb?" His face went blank, then his eyebrows met in the middle. Anger stiffened his features. "Fuck. Right. Okay, we'll deal with it."

"What's up?" Greg asked.

George sighed. "Are our passports up to date?"

Greg nodded. "Why…"

"Moon's got himself into a bit of bother in Amsterdam."

"Shit."

George stared Ichabod directly in the eye. "How do you feel about looking after The Cardigan Estate while we're gone?"

Feck me. I made it tae the top of the ladder.

Chapter Thirty-Four

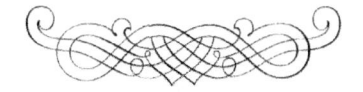

Moon took a moment to catch his breath. He'd be found soon unless he could get the hell out of here. Here was a room in an Amsterdam backstreet, a place he'd thought he'd been asked to go to so another offer could be put on the table. One that didn't sour his guts. Make him want to puke. But the offer from his previous visit had been repeated, and he'd said no again.

He should never have come back a second time. Should have left things as they were: him refusing to have anything to do with taking working girls out of the country to the UK. He wasn't into trafficking, which was what had been proposed, even though it had been dressed up as something nicer. Women would still need to pay a pimp a cut of their wages—Moon being that pimp, assigned by the man who'd ordered his incarceration here. Knowing what Debbie had been through, he wouldn't be walking down that path.

But if the twins didn't get here in time, he might have to show willing.

Hendrik Alderliesten was a cunning bastard. On the first trip, he'd plied Moon with booze and weed, the floating sensation reminding him of the good old days in his youth, where being reckless with your health was the norm. These days, he preferred to treat his body with more respect, bar his cigar smoking and a bit too much booze. Food, though; Debbie was a good cook and made sure he ate proper meals. Lots of veg and whatnot.

Fuck, he missed her.

His room here, a bare-walled prison with only a bed, toilet, and shower, was usually locked by some bloke called Bart, one of Hendrick's heavies. But a call from the boss himself when Bart had brought Moon some food meant Bart had run to see what the problem was, leaving the door unlocked, and the front door had slammed.

Moon had crept out, spotting a guard at the bottom of the stairs. In the past, when Moon had been fitter, he'd have gone down there and beat the shit out of him, then left the building. But the man held a gun, so Moon had sidled into the room next to his, an office of sorts. He'd found his phone in a desk drawer and messaged Debbie:

MOON: GET THE TWINS TO AMSTERDAM. TRAPPED. HENDRIK HAS TURNED NASTY.

He'd typed in the address, something he'd taken note of when he'd arrived.

DEBBIE: WHAT? OMG!

MOON: MIGHT NOT BE ABLE TO REPLY AGAIN. LOVE YOU.

That last bit had almost broken him, because he *did* love her. She'd become his life, his world, and he might never see her again.

The thought of that stung his eyes.

Sounds from downstairs had his heart rate banging on and on, then skipping a few beats. Pain under his ribcage brought him up short. Panic or heart attack? He debated whether to take his phone with him or put it back. He deleted the messages, pressed the OFF button, and slung it in the drawer.

Thuds on the stairs. Fuck, he needed to get back to his room.

He opened the door, reaching his in a second or two. But he'd left it too late. The crack of a gunshot barked, and he waited for the bullet to find it's mark.

Nothing happened. No pain, but a bullet hole marred the wall ahead.

"You were told you can't leave your room." Bart.

Moon turned to face him on the landing. "I heard noises, thought I could help. You know I'm a leader, that I can get shit sorted."

Bart laughed. "You're too old to deal with what we just had to. You've already admitted you rely on your men to do the dirty work for you. Do you have an answer for us yet?"

"I'll do it," Moon said. "I'll do whatever Hendrick wants."

He fucking wouldn't, but what choice did he have? If he wanted to get out of here and save those women, he'd have to pretend.

"Get in your room," Bart snapped. "I'll speak to Hendrick."

Moon stepped inside, the door closing behind him, the lock clicking into place.

I'm going to kill the fucking lot of them. Bastards.

To be continued in *Rijzen*,
The Cardigan Estate 27